Poetry and
Poets

A Luke Littlefield Mystery

Stephen E Stanley

Pottery and Poets
Stephen E Stanley
Copyright 2015

Printed in the United States of America
Stonefield Publishing 2015

Books by Stephen E Stanley

A MIDCOAST MURDER
A Jesse Ashworth Mystery

MURDER IN THE CHOIR ROOM
A Jesse Ashworth Mystery

THE BIG BOYS DETECTIVE AGENCY
A Jesse Ashworth Mystery

MUDER ON MT. ROYAL
A Jesse Ashworth Mystery

COASTAL MAINE COOKING
The Jesses Ashworth Cook Book

JIGSAW ISLAND
A Novel of Maine

DEAD SANTA!
A Jesses Ashworth Mystery

MURDER AT THE WINDSOR CLUB
A Jeremy Dance Mystery

UP IN FLAMES
A Jeremy Dance Mystery

ALL THE WAY DEAD
A Luke Littlefield Mystery

CRUISING FOR MURDER
A Jesse Ashworth Mystery

A GRAVE LOCATION
A Luke Littlefield Mystery

MURDER AND MISBEHAVIOR
A Jeremy Dance Mystery

Characters

Luke Littlefield- Anthropologist at Cranmore College, former catalogue model, Luke writes crime novels under the name of Danny Black.

Bryan Sullivan- former homicide detective for the West Hollywood Police Department, Bryan now owns an antique shop and takes on another job as well

Dustin Rodriguez- a public relations agent, Dustin is Luke's best friend.

Norma Jean Baker- octogenarian Norma Jean was once a stand in for Marilyn Monroe. Still man crazy after all these years.

Bert Higgins- Archeology professor at Cranmore College

Blake Carter- Photographer to the stars

Buffy Cunningham-plays the dumb blonde too hard.

Madison Smith- Luke's assistant

Richard Hall- anthropology graduate student and former military intelligence officer

Brad Tanner- funeral director from Maine, he's engaged to Madison.

Ian Stoddard- Scottish action hero movie star

The Followers:

Judy Johnson- not who she said she was

Amanda Springer- didn't know what she was getting into

Barbara and Joshua Levesque- owners of the Sky View Motel

And others:

Mary Brooks- Medical examiner

Max Bailey- FBI agent

Doug Connelly- FBI agent

Bruce Wilson and **David Preston**- Provincetown innkeepers

The Provincetown Poets:

James Cameron- gay fiction writer and poet

Buford Chase- nationally known reporter

Laurence Stafford- best-selling suspense novelist

Author's Note:

This book is a work of fiction. All characters, names, institutions, and situations depicted in the book are the product of my imagination and not based on any persons living or dead. Anyone who thinks he or she is depicted in the book is most likely delusional and should be institutionalized.

Stonefield Publishing
Portland, Maine
StonefieldPublishing@gmail.com

Author's Web page: **http://stephenestanley.com/**

Cape Cod 1690

Seven men gathered at the grave, all dressed in various styles of clothing. Women did not attend the burial. It was not the custom. John Dutton, the tallest of the men at nearly six feet, towered above the rest. Since the mysterious death of Reverend Josiah Babbage two days ago, he had taken on the role of religious leader.

"In so much as it hath pleased God to take our brother Josiah, it is our duty to question not the plan of Almighty God, but to humbly submit to God's judgment." Here John paused for effect.

Since the founding of the small fishing town six years ago, death had visited the little village eighteen times. English building techniques had proven inadequate for the harsh New England climate and many of the saints of the village had succumbed to illness. John Dutton, like most of the settlers, knew the Bible by heart, He continued with the words of the Gospel of John. "I am the resurrection, and the life, he that believeth in me, though he were dead, yet shall he live."

"Help! Oh, help!" cried ten year old Betty Brown, who burst onto the scene coming over the hill from the village.

"What means this, child?" asked one of the men. Little Betty was flushed and out of breath.

"Come, oh come!" she cried. "The village be on fire!"

The men took off on the run, forgetting the half buried Reverend Josiah as they sprinted. At the crest of the hill they saw the group of women and children coming to them. Off in the distance the flames were consuming the wooden stockade and the huts behind it.

"It were an attack by the Indians," said Mary Dutton to her husband. Tears were spilling down her cheek.

"We have been at peace with our Indian neighbors," replied John. "I cannot believe that they would attack us so."

"These were not our Indians," said Mary's sister Prudence, finding Mary and taking her hand. "These were Indians unknown to us."

"What are we to do, John," his wife sobbed as she watched her house go up in flames.

"We shall pray," said John as the villagers gathered around him looking for direction. "God will direct our next move."

Chapter 1

Buffy Cunningham sat in the front of my class filing her nails and painting them a bright shade of purple. Before I moved to California I thought the Valley Girl stereotype was just a cultural myth. After all I'm an anthropologist and I'm supposed to know about different cultures. As it turns out, valley girls are real, or so it seemed.

"Professor Littlefield, are we, like, going to study anything interesting?" Buffy was at this point holding up a mirror in front of her face with one hand and applying mascara with the other. The rest of the class suppressed giggles. As head of the anthropology department at Cranmore College, I usually don't teach the introductory classes, but we were shorthanded for the early summer term, and I decided to take a turn with Introduction to Cultural Anthropology myself. Big mistake. It was the middle of May and only students taking the short summer courses offered by the college remained.

"No, Buffy, we are not," I responded. The giggles in the class broke out into laughter. Buffy looked around and smiled thinking she had said something clever, not realizing that they were laughing at her, not with her.

"For Tuesday's assignment I want you to write a one page paper on the Nacirema tribe. Describe the typical day of a tribe member." In anthropology Nacirema is a term we use to examine, with detachment, the practices and the culture of North Americans. Nacirema is, of course, American spelled backwards. It's a great exercise for beginning students to view their own culture as someone outside the culture would. All of my students had figured out the assignment. All but one.

"Who are these people?" Buffy asked.

"It's a tribe in North America," I answered.

"Oh, Indians?"

"We call them Native American now, Miss Cunningham. I suggest you Google the name. See you all on Tuesday."

Several of the students gave me the thumbs up as they exited the classroom. Others just shook their heads. If nothing else Buffy Cunningham provided the comic relief.

"Hey Luke, buy a guy a cup of coffee?" asked Bryan Sullivan. Bryan and I have been going out for over a year. He had been a police officer here in West Hollywood before quitting the force and starting an antique store. Bryan is a muscular six feet four inches and has the dark good looks that make people take a second look. Today he was dressed in a campus security uniform with a lot of gold braid.

"Only if you explain why you are dressed like that. It's not even Halloween yet."

"Deal."

We walked about a block from the campus to a small coffee shop called The Coffee Break. This was the third name change of the place in two years. We walked in silence, ordered our coffee, and sat at a booth in the back of the café.

"The uniform," I said. "Explain."

"I miss police work and this position became available. I'm head of campus security."

"And this is the first time I'm hearing about it?"

"I wanted to surprise you. We'll be working at the same place."

"What about the antique shop?"

"It turns out I like managing the store and buying the antiques, but I don't like running the store."

"So who's running the store?"

"Norma Jean," he said smiling. "I thought you'd like me working here."

"I do, it just took me by surprise. I'm also surprised that Norma Jean hasn't blabbed the news before now."

"I had to threaten to put her in 'The Home,' but she got the message." Norma Jean Baker was somewhere in her eighties and still thought of herself as twenty. She claimed to have been a stand in for Marilyn Monroe. She still had the blonde hairstyle of the late Miss Monroe, but the rest of her had loosened and sagged with gravity and time. Norma Jean had long ago checked into Crazy Town and had never checked out.

"I need to get back to class," I said looking at my watch, "but when you come home tonight, be wearing the uniform. I have a case for you to work on."

"My favorite kind of case," he said and smiled.

Two days later I was sitting at my desk and looking at my calendar. Tomorrow was my birthday and it always reminded me to take stock of my life. I'm the head anthropologist at a small college in Southern California. I grew up in Maine. My parents were killed in a freak accident that left me orphaned and rich. I worked my way through college as a male underwear model, and since turning thirty I still got the occasional opportunity to model men's clothing for a prestigious catalogue company. I'm also the author of several crime novels and write under the name of Danny Black. I try very hard to keep the writing and modeling separate from my teaching career. I'm not sure the academic world would take me seriously if they knew I was a model and fiction writer.

Despite my varied resume, I've only had two boyfriends in five years. The first was with movie star Ian Stoddard. Ian was a great guy, but I just didn't fit into the whole movie star thing. My current love is Bryan Sullivan. Bryan is one of the best looking men around and that's saying something here in West Hollywood where pretty boys are a dime a dozen. But he's also one of the nicest and kindest guys around.

As professor Littlefield I dress in baggy clothes and wear dark framed glasses to try to look the part. I've always believed that no one would take me seriously as a scholar if I looked like an underwear model.

"And that," I said aloud as I picked up the calendar and tossed it across the room, "is my life."

"What was all that about?" asked Dean Babcock standing in the doorway watching me toss the calendar.

"Just taking stock of my life," I sighed. "Devoid of meaning."

"Most people would kill to have your life."

"I guess. I'm just wondering if I have any effect on the students at all."

"Let me guess," said Babcock. "It's Buffy Cunningham."

I looked up in surprise. "Buffy?"

"You're not the only professor she has. I've had a number of complaints."

"She is a challenge," I admitted.

"Don't worry. She won't last the semester."

"I'm not sure I will either," I said.

"Nonsense, of course you will."

"You didn't stop by just to give me a pep talk. What's up?"

"I have a possible project for you."

"If it's about relocating graves again, no thanks. That almost got me killed."

"No, nothing like that," he replied.

"Good."

"Not exactly anyway."

"What do you mean, not exactly?"

"A building is being torn down in Provincetown on Cape Cod. An old dump from colonial times was discovered under the building. This dump is a gold mine of colonial artifacts. The Cranmore College's archeology interns will be doing the excavation. This is a great opportunity for a California school. Professor Bert Higgins has asked for your help. They need someone to identify the artifacts and reconstruct daily life in Colonial Massachusetts. Your work with material culture is well known." I had published several articles on material culture, also known as artifacts, in one of the academic anthropological periodicals.

"Would I have to go there?" Going there would be awesome, but I didn't want to sound too enthusiastic until I heard more.

"At some point, yes. But the artifacts will be shipped here for you to examine."

"I have a pretty full class load," I said in mild protest. I really wanted to do this, but I didn't want to appear too eager.

"I'll get you a teaching assistant."

"My last teaching assistant was a criminal using my office for internet hacking."

"We have some of your previous grad students lined up. What do you say? You can hand over Buffy Cunningham to your TA."

"Tempting," I replied.

"And there is grant money."

"I'll take it," I said. I didn't want to play too hard to get for too long.

There was a red mustang, a black Ford SUV, and a green BMW parked in front of my house when I pulled into my driveway. Norma Jean Baker, Bryan Sullivan, and Dustin Ramirez were already inside preparing for my birthday. I had a momentary desire to get in my car and keep driving. The problem was that it was my house, and I had to come back sometime.

I was craving a nice thick steak, maybe with a baked potato and a side salad. Whatever they were cooking in my kitchen would be some vegan gluten free tofu creation. Oh boy.

"Happy Birthday," the three of them shouted out in unison.

"Thanks," I said. "Something smells good." That was a lie. It smelled like someone was boiling bars of soap.

"Quinoa salad and tofu scramble," said Norma Jean.

"Yum," I lied again. I was sure to go to hell. Bryan rolled his eyes. He was no fan of vegan cooking either. Suddenly I realized how everyone was dressed. Bryan had on a shirt and tie. The shirt was straining against his muscular chest. Dustin had on a bright red silk shirt and ironed slacks, and Norma Jean was wearing a strapless evening gown showing off her breasts, which reminded me of two dried and wrinkled grapefruits. It was not flattering.

"Why are you all dressed up?" I asked.

"Never mind," said Bryan. "Get out of those baggy clothes, comb your hair, lose the glasses and get into one of those Benson and Bloom suits you own."

"I've arranged for a professional photographer to take a group photo of us," added Dustin.

"A photographer?" I asked.

"Blake Carter," replied Dustin.

"Wow!" I was impressed. Blake Carter was the photographer to the stars. His works were featured in every major magazine and were shown in galleries across the country. "How did you get him?"

"I've worked with him. He has taken photos of some of my clients." Dustin had started his own public relations company last summer after a health scare. "And he's Richard's cousin." Richard Hall was one of my former grad students. He and Dustin had become an item when we all were working on grave relocations back in Brookfield, Maine.

Dustin's Latin good looks was hard to resist. If he wasn't my best friend, well you get the idea.

"That makes it handy," I remarked. "Where's my drink?"

"I've made a pitcher of cosmos for you assholes," said Norma Jean as she began pouring out the pink liquid into iced glasses.

"What's new with you?" Dustin asked Bryan. "I haven't seen you in weeks."

"I've taken a job as the head of campus security."

"Can't stay away from the police thing, huh? What about the antique shop?"

"Norman Jean is going to manage it for me."

"I'm a good manager, and it'll give me a chance to meet men. And if they're real nice to me I can take them into the back room and give 'em the works."

"Gross!" said Dustin covering his ears.

"Not in my shop!" gasped Bryan. "We're not zoned for that."

The doorbell rang saving us from further disturbing visual images.

"I'll get it," said Dustin. He returned with Blake Carter and introduced us all. Blake was in his late thirties, tall, blond with long bushy hair, and very good looking. He was the whole package.

"Pleased to meet you all," he said. "You look familiar," he said to me.

"Luke has done some modeling for *Benson and Bloom*."

"You're a model?" he asked in a surprised voice that almost bordered on insulting.

"Don't let the fancy suit and glasses fool you," said Bryan. "Under those clothes is one hot dude." He took out his wallet and pulled out a photo of me in just a towel.

"That's you?" he asked.

"I'm not liking the tone here," I said.

"Sorry, it's just the way you're dressed. I'd love to photograph you sometime."

"He means in the nude," added Dustin.

"He never shows his ding-a-ling," sighed Norma Jean.

"The world's loss," added Bryan.

"I could use some new stills," I said. Talking about my ding-a-ling wasn't appropriate birthday conversation. Everyone looked at me surprised. The truth is I like to model once in a while. It's good for the ego and I knew that at age thirty-two I didn't have much longer left. I'm very careful to keep my anthropology work separate from my writing and occasional modeling.

"Well," said Blake, "let's get started and get a group photo. And happy birthday by the way. Now if you'll all line up against the wall." We all lined up and posed for the picture.

"What's that smell?" asked Bryan.

We all looked to the kitchen where smoke was rolling out the door and setting off the smoke alarm. "Oh, my god!" yelled Dustin as he raced into the kitchen. "Dinner is burning."

"There is a God," I whispered to Bryan as I headed for the fire extinguisher.

Chapter 2

After the fire was put out and the air cleared in my kitchen we had all moved on to a new restaurant name Vegina. It was a new vegan café run by two lesbians. I like to eat out at different restaurants, but this place gave the term "eating out" a whole new disturbing image.

"If you all gather around the table I'll try to take another group photo," said Blake. "Luke, you get in the middle, Bryan you stand behind him and Norma Jean and Dustin on either side. And Luke for god's sake take off those glasses. That's good." He aimed the camera at us and we heard the click and saw the flash.

"Looks good," he said and sat back down.

"Vegina," repeated Norma Jean looking over the menu. "You know it sounds like…"

"Yes, we got that," I said interrupting her.

"And there's a lot of women here," she continued.

"We noticed," said Dustin.

"You don't think this is…"

"Are you ready to order?" asked a waitress covered with colorful tattoos and sporting a crew cut.

"I'll take the portabella mushroom burger on the gluten-free bun," said Norma Jean.

"I'll have the stuffed tomatoes with whirled soy beans," I said.

"I'll have the black bean burger," said Bryan.

"Same thing," said Blake nodding at Bryan.

"Stuffed tomatoes," said Dustin.

"Very good," said the waitress. "If you need anything just let me know."

"It seems to me that we don't see each other as much as we should. I had no idea your business was so busy," I said to Dustin.

"My PR clients are getting some good photo coverage," he replied.

"Just make sure your health doesn't suffer." Dustin had suffered exhaustion when he worked for a high pressure firm.

"Yes, mother."

"And what's new with you?" asked Dustin.

"I've got an offer to do some research on some archeological finds, and I'm getting a new teaching assistant."

"You could use one," said Bryan. "I know you had one that didn't work out."

"Didn't work out is an understatement," I replied.

"Where are these finds?" asked Norma Jean.

"Provincetown on Cape Cod." They all looked at me.

"Do you get to go there?" asked Dustin.

"At some point, yes."

"Count me in," said Dustin.

"Me too," added Norma Jean.

"And don't even think of going without me," said Bryan.

"I've always wanted to photograph the cape," said Blake. "I think I'd like to go, too. Maybe I could do a photo spread on your findings."

"Photographing the artifacts is an important job." I replied. "I can scrounge up some grant money."

"I'll do it *gratis*. I need the tax deductions."

"Road trip!" yelled Norma Jean.

"We are not driving to Massachusetts from California," I said. "We're flying. I don't even know when we will be going yet."

"Buzz kill," muttered Norma Jean.

"No parachute for you," Dustin said to her.

The air was hot and sticky in my office, and it seemed like the air conditioner wasn't keeping up with the heat. After growing up in northern Maine with its ten months of winter, I usually welcome being warm rather than cold, but today the air seemed stuffy.

I looked at the pile of papers on my desk and thought that maybe that was the reason I felt like I needed air. They were the first reports of my freshmen intro class, and I wasn't in the mood to wade through them yet. There was a knock on my door and a beautiful young lady was standing there.

"Madison! Come in and have a seat," I said standing up and pointing to the chair in front of my desk.

"It's good to see you Professor Littlefield."

"I thought you were in Maine with Brad?" Madison Smith was one of my graduate interns on the grave project in Maine. She fell in love with Brad Tanner, the local undertaker in Brookfield, Maine.

"I wanted to finish my graduate work and study with you. Brad hired someone to run the business in Brookfield and bought into a funeral home business here. We'll be in

Maine in the summer and out here in the winter, though he's thinking of selling the Maine business."

"That sounds perfect," I said. "I'm thrilled you'll be studying here."

"There's more," she said. "Dean Babcock called me into his office. He said you would be looking for a teaching assistant. I was hoping you would consider me."

"Are you sure you can put up with me?"

"I think I can work with you," she said with a mischievous look on her face. "I'm not so sure about Danny Black, though. He's a bad ass." My grad students on the project had figured out my double life. I had threatened them with disappearing transcripts if they said a word to anyone.

"Danny Black *is* a bad ass," I replied. "But I don't think you'll see much of him. See that desk over there?"

"Yes," she said looking at the desk on the other side of the office.

"Take this pile of papers over there and start grading them. I'm going out for coffee."

"I got the job?"

"Yes, God help you. You are my new teaching assistant."

"So this is your new hangout?" I asked Bryan as I walked into the security office. There were TV monitors everywhere and officers sitting at a large console watching the campus activities.

"Yes and I have my own private office, unlike the West Hollywood PD." We walked into his office and I sat in a chair in front of his desk

"I never even noticed the cameras around campus."

"That's the idea. We don't want to appear too intrusive. Just enough for everyone to know we're here."

"What happened to your predecessor?"

"He got snapped up by a high end private security firm for twice the salary."

"Good for him," I remarked.

"And good for me. This is a dream job."

"A dream job?"

"Whenever I get bored I can watch you walk across campus. That's a nice ass to watch."

"Easy there," I said feeling my face turn red. "What's the down side?"

"The down side is that I'll have to be here some weekends."

"I see," I said. "How many weekends?"

"Not many. Mostly my second in command can handle things."

"I have some news. You remember Madison?"

"Of course, smart and lovely."

"She's my new teaching assistant."

"Excellent. She's a winner. What do you want to do about dinner?"

"I want to avoid anything with tofu in it."

When I got back in the office Madison was still working on grading the papers.

"Do you want to double check my grading?" she asked.

"I trust you to grade them. I do want to see Buffy Cunningham's paper when you get to it. The girl is a complete airhead."

"Here it is," she said taking it out of the file of corrected papers. "It's very good."

"It's what?" I asked.

"It's very good. Here take a look," she handed me the paper. It was very good. In fact it was excellent. Buffy Cunningham would have a lot to explain. "Do you think she plagiarized?"

"It's possible of course, but I don't think so."

I looked it over again. "I agree. It's a good first effort, but it isn't perfect. It shows a good background knowledge and some original thoughts. I think she might be playing us."

"The word on campus is that she's dumber than a stump."

"That was my assessment, too," I said as I handed the paper back to her.

Buffy Cunningham was texting on her phone during my class. I was introducing Madison to the class and explaining the role of teaching assistant. Without waiting to be called on she blurted out, "You mean this chick is going to be our teacher?"

"Miss Smith is going to be my teaching assistant," I said. "And your use of the word chick, Miss Cunningham, is offensive."

"Dude, don't get on my case. I got issues."

"See me after class Miss Cunningham."

"I don't usually date teachers," she said, "but you're kind of cute." There was nervous tittering among the students.

"Miss Smith will be with us," I responded.

"I'm not into three ways." Now there was outright laughter in the room.

"That will be enough, Miss Cunningham. Now as I was saying before these disturbing intrusions Miss Smith and I will be both teaching this course." I gave them a brief summary of Madison's credentials, that she would be receiving her doctorate in a few weeks, and how she was instrumental in the Brookfield, Maine project."

"Miss Cunningham, can you explain to me how you managed to write such a good first paper when you appear to be totally uninterested in my class?" Buffy was sitting in my office. Madison was at her desk on the other side of the room and I had left the door open."

"You got me there, Professor," she said. She had dropped her valley girl affectations. "Maybe I overdid it."

"What do you mean?" I asked confused. She got up and closed the door to my office. She threw a wallet with an ID card and a badge on my desk.

"I'm FBI special agent Marie Cunningham. Buffy is my nickname. I'm here investigating some criminal activity on campus."

"I see. Who else knows?" What the hell is going on?

"Dean Babcock and now you and Madison. We've checked you both out and you can be trusted."

My head was spinning from this turn of events. "Does campus security know?" I asked.

"I understand Chief Sullivan is your boyfriend, so I've let him know, but not the other security guards because they could be involved,"

"Involved in what?" asked Madison.

"All in good time. I'll let you know when I think you should. Now if you will excuse me I have a dorm party to go to."

"Any ideas about what's going on?" I asked Madison after Buffy or Marie or whoever the hell she was left the office.

"No idea at all. I haven't heard any rumors about anything. If I had to guess I'd say it involves drugs."

"I would think that too, except the FBI isn't usually interested in college drug use. Unless of course it was some high level operation."

"Well, I'll keep my ear to the ground," said Madison as she picked up the pile of papers and began recording the grades.

Chapter 3

Sullivan Antiques and Collectables sits on Wolfgang Street next to a beauty shop named Curl Up and Dye. Located on the other side of the shop is Red's Rugged Gym, an upscale establishment that caters to the beautiful people.

I stepped through the door of Bryan's shop and a chime sounded to let the clerk know that a customer had entered.

"Oh, it's you," said Norma Jean stepping out of the back room.

"Nice greeting," I answered.

"Sorry, I thought it might be the nice older gentleman who stopped by this morning and said he'd be back. He was a hot one."

"Have you noticed that men who go out with you often die shortly after?"

"Can't help it if they have a bad heart. At least they get some before they go to the morgue."

"Bryan's got some nice stuff here," I observed looking around. I hadn't been here for a few weeks.

"He's got good taste," said Norma Jean. I noticed that she tried to keep my attention on her so I wouldn't look around. Whenever I moved she moved in front of me. Suspecting something was up I jumped two feet to the left of her and then I saw what she was trying to hide.

"What the hell!" I yelled. On the wall was a sign that said "Vintage Poster" and it was a full size poster of me wearing only a pair of Benson and Bloom white briefs. The poster had been made to look old.

"I had a bunch of them made up," said Norma Jean pointing to the poster. "It's selling very well to all the gay guys and some of the women as well."

"That is not an antique," I said fuming. "And I'm not a vintage model."

"Maybe not yet. This here is what we call marketing. Give the people what they want. They're going for a hundred dollars a pop."

"How much?"

"One hundred George Washingtons."

"Does Bryan know you're doing this?"

"Well, not exactly."

"Then exactly what does he know?"

"He knows I have some vintage posters of male models."

"And he knows the model is me?"

Just then two middle age men came into the shop and began looking around. I pretended to pick up several pieces of china and examined the marking on the back. Norma Jean grabbed a newspaper and pretended to read it, except of course that it was upside down.

"Hey Jim, look at this," said the taller of the two men.

"That's hot," said the other as he walked across the store and joined his partner at the poster. He picked up the price tag and looked at it. "Let's get this."

"We can get it framed and hang it in the bedroom."

"Grab it before someone else gets it."

Norma Jean came over and whispered in my ear, "I'll give you a cut on all I sell."

"Deal," I said.

"I checked out the shop today," I said to Bryan as we ate lunch at the school's cafeteria. It was late afternoon and there weren't many students there. "Norma Jean seems to be enjoying the shop."

"Okay," said Bryan, "What did she do?"

"She was waiting for a gentleman to return," I said. "She said he was hot."

"That woman is tripping."

"How's the new job?"

"It's great. Much like police work on an easy day."

"So why is the FBI here?" I asked. Bryan almost choked on his coffee.

"You know about that?"

"Yes, I was about to kick Buffy Cunningham out of my class when she told me she was working undercover."

"Do you know about the Clery Act?"

"I've never heard of it," I said.

"The Clery Act was an act placed into law by the U.S. Congress. It requires all colleges and universities that receive federal monies to disclose information about crimes on or near campuses. There are penalties against institutions for infractions."

"And what does that have to do with Cranmore College?"

"I asked the FBI for help. I looked through the files and found several unreported cases of violence against students. I want to make sure that we are in compliance."

"You mean your predecessor under-reported campus crime?"

"I don't think so, at least not on purpose. He reported campus crime, but not crimes against students from the community." Just then his cell phone went off. He read the text message. "Speaking of crime, I have to go. See you at home."

Brad Tanner, young and handsome, and dressed in a gray suit, walked into my office.

"Dr. Littlefield, it's good to see you," he said and smiled.

"Good to see you, too. Madison told me you had moved out here." I got up and shook his hand.

"Madison really wanted to finish school out here, and I wasn't sad to leave Maine for the winter."

"I'm glad you've both come back, and I'm thrilled that she's become my teaching assistant."

"She's thrilled to work with you. That's all she talks about. If I didn't know better, I'd be jealous," he laughed.

"Madison's not here, I think she's working on her dissertation. Why don't the two of you come over for dinner tonight?" I jotted down my address and passed it to him.

"That would be great."

"I'll call the others and we'll have a little reunion."

"Awesome," he looked at his watch. "I need to get back to the funeral home. We have a service to get ready for."

"Great. See you around seven."

I phoned Norma Jean and Dustin and invited them over. After I hung up the phone I realized that I didn't have any food in the house or any idea what to make. Time to head to the store.

I had uncorked a bottle of red wine, placed a pan of vegetable lasagna in the oven, and was putting together a salad when I heard a car pull up in front of my house.

Norma Jean was the first to arrive. She was wearing a pink track suit that had been bedazzled with rhinestones, white sneakers, and a pink headband.

"Going jogging?" I asked.

"Not till I get a new boob job. These puppies flap around too much."

"Too much information. How's business?"

"I sold two more of those posters. We have a gold mine."

"I think you better tell Bryan what you're doing."

"Bryan gets his money…"

The doorbell rang and I knew it was Brad and Madison. No one else would bother to use the doorbell.

"You remember Norma Jean," I said to them.

"How could we forget," said Madison as she gave her a hug.

I excused myself and went into the kitchen to check on dinner. Dustin arrived and joined me in the kitchen.

"Need any help?"

"You can slice that loaf of bread over there."

"Sure thing. Dinner smells good."

"Now fess up. I haven't seen you with Richard for weeks. What's going on?" Richard hall is an ex-military officer and one of my best graduate students. Dustin had met Richard on a project in Maine that I headed last summer.

"Okay, Richard dumped me."

"What do you mean he dumped you? Did you guys break up?"

"No, he just stopped returning my calls. I texted him, called him, nothing."

"That's rather odd, isn't it? If he wanted to break up with you why not just say so?"

"That's what I thought."

"Did you go to his apartment?"

"No, I didn't want to appear too needy."

"Did it ever cross your mind," I asked with as much patience as I could muster, "that he might be in trouble?"

"You think that could be it?"

"Bryan!" I yelled. "Get in here."

"What's up?" asked Bryan as he entered the kitchen. I gave him a quick summary of the situation. "First thing tomorrow we need to go over to his place and do a wellness check."

"A wellness check?" asked Dustin.

"It's when the police are contacted by a concerned relative or neighbor that something might be wrong," explained Bryan.

"But you're not a policeman anymore," Dustin stated.

"I'm campus security and Richard is a Cranmore student, so I have the right to check on him," Bryan explained.

"Is that true?" I asked.

"More or less."

"More or Less?"

"I don't think it will be a issue."

"Well, I think dinner is ready," I said. "We'll sort it all out tomorrow."

Chapter 4

Dustin, Bryan and I met for breakfast before heading over to Richard's apartment. We called Richard's cell phone as well as his home number and both calls went to voice mail. His home voicemail was full, which meant that he had been a way for some time.

"Did he say anything about going on a trip or anything?" Bryan asked Dustin.

"No, in fact he told me he had very little money for travel. I offered to give him some but he refused."

"What about any family?" I asked.

"He has a married sister up in Sacramento."

"Do you know her name?" asked Bryan.

"Susan Sutter."

I pulled out my smart phone and did a search for Susan Sutter. It didn't take long to track her down. She appeared to be one of those people who live their life on line. I took a chance and sent her a message on a social media site. She responded right away. No, she hadn't heard from him and no she didn't know if he had gone somewhere."

"I'm really worried now," said Dustin. "I thought it was his way of breaking up with me. But he could be in trouble."

"One more coffee refill," said Bryan, "and we're on our way."

Richard lived about a half mile from campus in a graduate housing apartment owned by the college. It was a simple concrete block building, but it was clean if sparse.

Bryan was wearing his campus security uniform and took out a pass keycard to the front door. We climbed the stairs to the third floor and knocked on the apartment door.

There was no answer. Bryan took out another key card and slid it into the lock. We entered the apartment; the shades had been pulled shut and it was dark. I reached over to the light switch and flipped the lights on. What we saw wasn't comforting.

"This place has been tossed," said Bryan. We looked around, and it was clear that someone had been in the apartment and looking for something. But where was Richard?

"I'll take it from here," said a voice behind us. We turned around to see Buffy Cunningham standing in the door with two members of the local police force.

"What's going on?" asked Bryan. "What business does the FBI have with a missing grad student?"

"You're on a need-to-know basis. All you need to know is that Richard Hall was working with us and his disappearance is, well let's just call it unsettling."

"Richard works for the FBI?" asked Dustin stunned. "This isn't happening."

"Perhaps you better explain why the three of you are here," suggested Buffy Cunningham.

"This is Dustin Ramirez," said Bryan, "Richard's friend. Dustin is a good friend of ours, and he was worried that he hadn't heard from Richard for a while. As head of campus security I have the right to check on the students."

"When was the last time you heard from Richard?" Buffy addressed Dustin.

"We had lunch on Monday. I called him later in the day and only got voice mail. I sent text messages and never got a response."

"Was that usual? Did he often not answer?" she asked.

"He always answered or called back shortly," answered Dustin.

"That was three days ago," said Buffy. "Why did you wait for so long to check on him?"

"I thought he was breaking up with me," said Dustin in a weak voice.

"I see," said Buffy. I didn't like the way she said that.

"No need for the tone of judgment, Miss Cunningham," I said to her.

"Any idea where he could be?" she asked ignoring my comment. Bryan gave her the information we had from the phone call we made to the sister.

"I'll put out a BOLO on his car," she said.

"BOLO?" I asked.

"Be on the lookout. Now I think you three boys better run along and let us do our job. See you in class Dr. Littlefield."

"I don't like her," snarled Dustin when we left Richard's apartment.

"No one does," I said and then explained that she was in my class undercover and had taken on the persona of a particularly annoying young lady.

"I don't understand what he was doing for the FBI," said Dustin. "He never said anything to me about that."

"My guess is he didn't want to involve you whatever it was," said Bryan trying to smooth Dustin's feelings.

"I can't imagine what it was," I remarked.

"As soon as the FBI clears out of Dustin's apartment," suggested Bryan, "I suggest we go back and have a look on our own. Maybe we can figure it out. After all Dustin's more familiar with the place than the FBI. He might notice something missing or something that doesn't belong."

The FBI had done a thorough search of the apartment. What had been tossed in Richard's apartment had been re-tossed as far as we could tell.

"What a mess," said Dustin as he looked around.

"Why don't we tidy up the place," I suggested. "That way you might notice something amiss."

We busied ourselves putting the apartment back in order; that is as much as we could guess where things went.

"His laptop is here," said Dustin as he tried to organize Richard's desk. "But his USB drive isn't here." Dustin turned on the laptop and it opened up to the email program. "Looks like the FBI already checked his email."

"Take a look anyway," said Bryan. "You know best who he would be emailing."

"Look what I found in the dirty laundry basket," I said.

"Are those ladies' panties?" asked Bryan.

"Looks like it," I said holding it by my thumb and forefinger as far from me as I could.

"Apparently the FBI either didn't notice it or didn't think it significant," said Bryan. "Assholes probably think gay men like to wear panties."

"I'm sure some do," I said. "But I doubt that's one of Richard's fetishes." I looked to Dustin.

"Definitely not his thing," said Dustin wrinkling up his nose.

"Then this bedding," I said picking up a blanket off the living room floor, "could have come from the sofa and not the bedroom. Someone may have been staying here with Richard."

"Richard doesn't drink rum does he?" asked Bryan holding up a dirty glass and smelling it.

"He hates rum."

I went into the kitchen and rummaged in the trash can and pulled out an empty rum bottle. Clearly Richard had a guest.

"And this isn't my toothbrush," said Richard coming out of the bathroom.

"It appears," said Bryan with a wicked grin, "that Buffy Cunningham is a hack."

Norma Jean Baker was wearing a blue Japanese kimono and I suspected no underwear as she bustled about in my kitchen. Why my house became the preferred dining venue of our weekly vegetarian feast, I had no idea.

"What are you making?" I asked tentatively. I think I've already expressed my feelings about tofu inspired cuisine.

"Vegetable sushi," she replied. I watched her roll and cut the sushi. I had to admit this might not be too bad.

"Looks good," I said. "What's new with you?" I hadn't seen her for a few days.

"I got me a new man. He's a hot one and he's got some money, too."

"And?" There was always something more with her men.

"Well. He's married."

"Married?"

"It's cool. His wife is in the nursing home. She's gaga. She told him before she went into the home that he should enjoy life."

"Interesting," I said. That sounded like a line to me. But then again if any man wanted to take on Norma Jean, well, let's just say prayers would be in order.

"Where are the boys?"

"Dustin had to finish a conference call, and Bryan had to catch up on paperwork since the FBI are looking over the college."

"And what business does the FBI have with a small college?"

"Well, supposedly they're looking into the reporting of crimes on campus. A law was passed that colleges had to report major crimes."

"Major crimes at Cranmore?"

"I think that's just an excuse. I have an undercover agent in my class. I don't think they use undercover agents to check up on security paperwork."

"And Dustin's boyfriend is involved with the FBI?"

"Apparently, yes.

"Something is rotten in West Hollywood."

"It's rotten as hell," said Dustin stepping into the kitchen. I hadn't heard him come in. He looked terrible. I surmised that he hadn't slept for days.

"He probably has a very good reason for taking off," said Norma Jean, trying to cheer Dustin up. "Luke and Bryan will figure it out."

"You think so?"

"Yes, I do. Don't you Luke?"

"Yes," I answered. I wasn't so sure, but what else could I say? "There's Bryan now."

I heard the front door open and Bryan appeared in the kitchen door. "Evening all. I just signed for a package for you. I think it must be the artifacts from Cape Cod."

"Where did you leave them?" I asked.

"I put them in your office on your desk."

"Perfect."

"So what's cooking?" He asked tentatively.

"Sushi," said Norma Jean.

"I guess the kimono should have been a clue," replied Bryan.

"Some detective," sniffed Norma Jean.

"Some Geisha," responded Bryan.

Chapter 5

The special delivery box was sitting on my desk when I entered the office the first thing in the morning. The word 'fragile' was printed across the top and so I carefully picked it up to test its weight. I suppressed the urge to shake the package, though. I took the box over to my examination table and covered the table surface with white paper. Carefully I took a letter opener and slit open the box. The box was full of plastic packing material. I reached in and was able to lift out three objects, each wrapped in tissue and wrapped again in plastic bubble wrap.

"Good morning professor."

I turned around. Madison was heading to her desk. "Good morning Madison; I didn't hear you come in."

"You seemed intent on what you were doing."

"These are the first artifacts from the Cape Cod excavation." Madison came over to the table and looked over my shoulder as I unwrapped the first object.

"It's a clay pipe," she said looking at the object as I carefully placed it on the table.

"Yes, it's one of the most common objects from colonial times. Smoking was a relatively new pastime. Both men and women smoked. Note that this one is whole, complete with a long stem. Stems got broken off until there was barely any stem left. They had the name 'nose warmers' when the stem got down almost to the bowl."

"Can you tell the age?"

"Tobacco was expensive in the late 1600s.The bowls were small and narrow. As tobacco got cheaper the bowls became wider and deeper." I went to my desk and came back with a measuring tape. "The bowl size suggests this was made prior to the early 1700s. My guess is somewhere around 1670 to 1690."

I was about to pick up the second object when I heard the office door fly open. Madison and I spun around to face a very excited Bryan Sullivan.

"Dustin just received a text from Richard."

"What did the text say?" I asked.

"I'm fine. Don't worry about me."

"That's it?"

"That's it. Dustin tried to call the number but the phone was off."

"Was it from Richard's phone?"

"No, according to the FBI it was from a burner phone."

"What's a burner phone?" asked Madison.

"A prepaid phone. You pay cash and there is no record," I explained.

"How do we even know it was from Richard?"

"We don't, though the FBI are sure. The wording is some type of code."

"Code for what?"

"Agent Buffy wouldn't say."

"Agent Buffy," I said, "needs a good slap."

"I don't disagree with you there," said Bryan with a smile. "Well, I'll let you get back to work. If there is anything new I'll let you know."

"Lunch?"

"Cafeteria at noon."

"See you then."

It was sloppy joe day at the school cafeteria, and while there were other healthier choices on the menu, I chose to ignore them and enjoyed the ground beef entrée.

"I know what's going on," said Bryan as we sat at a small table in the corner. While the Cranmore College Cafeteria was a step above a hospital cafeteria, it couldn't be classified as cozy and warm.

"Going on where?"

"At the antique store. I know about the posters."

"I didn't doubt that you did," I said between bites. "Norma Jean needs watching."

"Norma Jean is as crazy as she is old."

"And I hope I'm that crazy when I'm that old."

"I'm sure you will be," said Bryan with a twinkle in his eye. "You've got a good start."

"Looks like you won't be having sex for a while."

"Like you could hold out for more than twenty-four hours."

"True," I admitted. "Now tell me what's really going on."

"Okay, but you can't tell anyone."

"Spill it."

"The FBI believes there is a terrorist cell here at the college."

"A terrorist cell? That's a little farfetched don't you think? We don't even have a political club here."

"It's not a political terrorist group," he said pushing back his empty plate, "It's a religious terrorist group."

"A what?"

"It's a group of nut jobs who believe we are in the last days and that everyone must believe as they do. They are out to create a Christian nation. The FBI believes they are going to do something drastic to bring attention to their cause."

"Have these people ever read a history book? People even in the time of Jesus believed that they were living in the end times. The world has had much darker times and we're still here."

"Logic and religion don't always go together."

"What has any of this to do with Richard?"

"Richard was working undercover as a possible recruit."

"Now it all makes sense. Does this group have a name?" I asked.

"They call themselves The Followers."

"So do you think Richard was discovered and that's why he disappeared?"

"Most likely."

"Why would he do it?"

"For the money. He's a grad student. Also he's ex-military and a great find for the FBI."

"So what do we do?" I asked with no ideas in mind.

"Let's just wait and see," said Bryan.

"Look at this," said Madison unwrapping the final artifact from the package. "It's some type of flask."

"This is a rare find. Glass objects were expensive in colonial times and this," I said turning it over in my hands, "is obviously hand-blown. It's unusual to find glass objects still intact."

"This is all from one site?"

"Yes, it's from an area between Truro and Provincetown. Most likely a small fishing settlement, and I think this must be from a dump site." So far we had a clay pipe, a powder horn that was intricately carved, and this glass flask. "Hopefully they'll be sending more artifacts along."

"How old do you think the site is?"

"Provincetown was the first stopping off area for the Pilgrims in 1620. It was there that they wrote the Mayflower Compact. They moved on to Plymouth, but the place was a fishing area for many years and slowly fishermen built cabins and settled in the area."

"And we get to go there?"

"Yes, I've been in contact with the archeological team. They'd like us to recreate what daily life was like in the late 1600s in that area."

"So we use the artifacts to examine material culture?"

"Exactly. I can't wait."

The door to my office flew open and agent Buffy Cunningham stood in the doorway.

"You really need to stop making dramatic entrances," I said somewhat annoyed.

"We found Richard Hall," she said.

"That's great," I said.

"Not for him it isn't. You'd better come along with me."

Chapter 6

Bryan and I tried to reach Dustin, but he wasn't answering his phone and we didn't want to leave a message other than 'please call.' Buffy Cunningham drove with Bryan and me as passengers. The ride to the hospital seemed to take forever. Buffy was on the phone talking with other agents.

"I see," she said. "I'll tell them."

"Tell us what?" asked Bryan.

"Richard is the victim of a hit and run accident."

"Where?" I asked.

"Apparently he was crossing the street from the Sky View Motel to the convenience store when he was hit."

"The Sky View Motel?" I asked. The Sky View was one of those hotels for divorced dads. "What was he doing there?"

"Hiding out would be my guess," said Buffy.

"Hiding from what?" asked Bryan.

"That's a good question. We'll have to ask him when he comes out of the emergency room."

"How bad are the injuries?" Bryan asked.

"Serious enough. We'll get more information when we see the doctor."

As it turned out Richard was being evaluated, and we ended up in the waiting room. Buffy tried using her credentials to get information, but the hospital staff was unimpressed. Dustin finally caught up with us and came rushing into the waiting room.

"What happened," he asked looking panicked. We told him all we knew. "What was he doing in a motel?"

"We'll have to ask him when he's able to tell us," said Buffy Cunningham. Buffy's cell phone went off and she spoke briefly. She hung up and walked back to where we were all sitting.

"There's been a development," she said.

"What is it?" asked Bryan. I could tell by the look on his face that he didn't like the sound of it.

"There's a dead woman in the room where Richard Hall was registered."

"What?" I asked incredulously.

"The body of a dead woman was found in Richard's room. What part of that did you not understand?"

"There must be an explanation," I said trying to come to terms with the news.

"The local police are working with the FBI to identify the woman. Hopefully Richard will be able to help," said Buffy more kindly that before.

Just then the doctor came in. We all stopped talking and looked at him.

"Mr. Hall is in stable condition. He's suffering from internal injuries as a result of the accident. We'll be keeping him here for a few days' observation."

"We need to speak with him now," said Buffy assuming her tough agent persona.

"Mr. Hall has been heavily sedated and may not have visitors until tomorrow," he answered. I got the feeling that he enjoyed pulling rank on the FBI agent.

"I'm putting a guard outside his door," she responded.

"You do that," said the doctor as he spun on his heels and left. I thought I heard the word 'bitch' being mumbled as he left, but maybe it was just wishful thinking on my part.

"Come on Dustin," I said. "Let's go. There's nothing you can do here. We'll be back tomorrow.

I had an early morning class and it was too early in the semester to have Madison take over entirely. Buffy Cunningham was seated in front of the class continuing, I guess, her undercover work. She had toned down her dumb blonde routine a bit, but not much.

"How long do you want this paper?" she asked just after I had given the class the requirements.

"Short enough to be interesting and long enough to cover the basics," I responded. I had just told the class a minimum of two pages and not more than five.

"You know there's a campus party this weekend, right?"

"I did not know, nor do I care. You are here to learn, not party," I said trying to sound like a professor. I was throwing Buffy a 'knock it off' look.

"Whatever," she said as I dismissed the class. As soon as all the students were gone she came up to me. "We're going to the hospital now to talk to Richard if you want to come along."

"Let's go," I said.

"How are you feeling?" asked Bryan as Richard sat in his hospital bed.

"Like I got hit with a truck," he said trying to smile, but gave a grimace as he shifted in his bed. "The pain meds help, but it still hurts."

"So tell us what happened," said Buffy taking out a note pad. "You better start at the beginning."

Richard looked at Bryan and me.

"You may speak in front of them," said Buffy. "They already know you are working with us."

"What about Dustin?" he asked.

"We'll decide what he needs to know as we go along. Right now he's more worried about you than curious about what you're doing."

"Okay," said Richard letting out what sounded like a sigh. "I've been attending the meetings of The Followers. The group seems to be made up of some undergrad and grad students here on campus. There are several groups in other west coast colleges as well, and a lot of others who feel disenfranchised by modern society."

Buffy nodded her head. She already knew this information and this was clearly for our benefit.

"There seems to be an inner core of believers and then the rest of us recruits. Judy Johnson, a member of the inner group, came to me for help. She said the group was planning something big and she wanted nothing to do with it. She wanted me to help her expose the group. She came to my apartment, but she received a text threatening her if she didn't return to the group. She wanted to hide somewhere, so she and I set up in the motel."

"And you didn't tell us any of this?" asked Buffy.

"It all happened so fast and I was trying to get more information to give to you."

"Go ahead with the story," she said.

"We set up at the motel where we registered under false names. We thought we were safe. Yesterday I went out for food and when I came back there was a dead girl in the room."

"Was it Judy Johnson?" asked Buffy.

"No, I never saw the girl before."

"Where was Judy then?" asked Bryan.

"Gone and now that I think about it her stuff was gone, too. Anyway when I saw the body I ran out of the room. I went to call the FBI and when I was crossing the street a car came out of nowhere and hit me."

"And they didn't stop?" I asked.

"No, and I had the feeling they were deliberately trying to run me over."

"What did the car look like?" asked Bryan. Buffy gave him a look as if to say she was supposed to ask the questions.

"Four door Chevy sedan. It was black and there were two women inside, I think."

"License plate?" asked Buffy.

"I couldn't tell, but it wasn't a California plate."

"Okay," said Buffy Cunningham recapping. "You made contact with Judy Johnson, who is a member of the Followers inner circle. You learned from her that they are planning a big event. She claimed that she wanted out, so you helped hide her in a local motel. You went out for food, came back, she was gone and the body of an unknown female was in your room. You ran out of the room and got hit by a car that you think was trying to run you down?"

"Yes," said Richard. "That's what happened."

"Then we need to do three things," said Buffy picking up her phone to make a call. "We need to find

Judy Johnson, we need to identify the dead girl, and we need to find out what this big event is going to be before someone else gets killed."

Norma Jean Baker was throwing objects around the shop clearly upset about something.

"What's going on?" I asked.

"That asshole doctor said I was too old for a boob job."

"Exactly how old did you tell him you were?" I asked.

"I gave him my real age. I told him I was sixty."

"That was your real age twenty-five years ago," I said. "No wonder he won't do it. You lied."

"A lady never tells her age."

"Except to her doctor," I answered.

"But that was my real age."

"*Was* is the correct tense. Anyway we have more important issues to deal with than your saggy boobs." I went on and gave her an update about Richard.

"Oh my. And that all happened in the last two days?"

"Yes, and the FBI agents are scrambling around trying to get answers."

"It sounds like he was set up."

"I think that's what the FBI is thinking, too. We won't have any more information until the FBI identifies the dead girl."

"Never a dull moment with you guys is there?"

"Nope, I guess not."

Chapter 7

Madison Smith looked up from her desk as I came into the office. "There's another package for you from the dig. This is exciting, sort of like Christmas."

"And a jigsaw puzzle," I replied. "We get to put little pieces together and hope we can see a bigger picture of daily life in colonial Cape Cod." I then gave her an update about Richard. They had been friends ever since the field work that my interns had done in Maine.

"Oh, I'm glad. I was worried. He doesn't seem like the type to disappear."

"Remember he's been trained by the military, and he was recruited by the FBI, so you know he takes his job seriously."

"I don't doubt it."

"Now, let's take a look at what the Provincetown dig has sent us."

I carefully began to open the package which was much larger than the previous one that Professor Higgins sent to me. The package contained two objects. The first was an earthenware pitcher about eight inches high and of a deep red-brown color. It seemed to be in almost perfect condition. The second object was a blue and white dish about six inches in diameter and quite chipped.

"This appears to be a cream pitcher, locally made earthenware," I said as Madison jotted down the information. "Earthenware, the texture is fine. Earthenware was locally produced and relatively inexpensive. Earthenware is a lesser quality than stoneware.

"The dish is Delft, a white background with blue designs. The design seems to be a European village scene. Delft is a tin glazed clay and is a general term, though most was made in Holland. Tin glazed ware was never made in Colonial America and was imported. It was expensive and chipped or broke easily and because of that it went out of favor by the early 1700s."

"Professor Higgins and his students must be in heaven," Madison sounded somewhat envious, I thought.

"California has some older settlement from the Spanish, but this is a rare opportunity to look at Colonial village life. Bert Higgins sent some notes and photos with this, if you wouldn't mind filing them."

"Will do."

"Tonight is vegetarian night at my house if you and Brad would like to come."

"I'll have to check with him, but I think we're free. What time?"

"Come around six," I said as my phone rang. It was Dustin.

"Luke," he said sounding out of breath. "They've just arrested Richard for the murder of that girl."

"What the hell are you doing?" Bryan was yelling at Buffy Cunningham and her two assistant agents, whose names we hadn't learned. We were in the college security office. "You know Richard didn't kill that girl."

"Get a grip, Sullivan," Buffy held up her hand. "Richard didn't kill anyone. But he was set up and we want to find out who did it and why. We want it to look like their plan worked and in order to do so we have to make it appear that the police think Richard is guilty."

"I see," said Bryan relaxing a bit. "Any progress?"

"We're checking out some leads," she answered.

"So basically nothing then?"

"Not yet, no."

"But you believe that all this is tied up with the religious terrorist group?" I asked.

"Most likely, but we need to find the link."

"And that link is the dead girl?" I asked.

"We're looking at missing persons reports right now," she said not really answering my question.

"I'm having a small get-together at my house for dinner tonight. If you're not busy come on over."

Buffy looked at me like I was some interesting insect she found crawling up her leg, then she relaxed. "Sure, why not."

"Six o'clock," and I wrote down my address.

"Are you freaking crazy?" asked Bryan after Buffy left the office.

"Getting information from Buffy is going to be easier if we're nice to her."

"I guess, but it's going to be hard."

"Alcohol helps."

Dustin was busy in my kitchen trying, I think, to forget about Richard's arrest. Buffy had taken him aside and explained to him that Richard was not really under arrest. Norma Jean was running around the house keeping everyone's wine glass filled up.

"How are things?" I asked Brad Tanner as he took his refilled wine glass and headed to the sofa where Madison was seated.

"I'm selling the Maine business and staying out here for good. This last winter was a killer."

"I don't blame you," I agreed. "And you have a pretty good incentive to stay here," I looked at Madison who blushed.

"That's for sure."

"Young love," sighed Norma Jean. "Though there's something to be said for maturity."

"How do you stay so young?" asked Madison.

"Good food, exercise, and sex," said Norma Jean with a wink. "And I'll bet this guy will run you ragged in that department." Both Brad and Madison blushed at that.

"Anyway," I said trying to change the subject. "I'm flying out to the East Coast next week."

"When did that come about?" asked Dustin bringing in a tray of cheese and crackers.

"I got a phone call this afternoon from the Provincetown dig. I'll be there for a few days."

"I thought we were all going," said Norma Jean.

"This will be just an initial trip to familiarize me with the area. I'll be going back again later to stay for a few weeks. You all can come and visit then."

"Are you going with him this time?" Madison asked Bryan.

"No, I can't leave the job just now. I've only just started."

Buffy was seated on the sofa when her cell phone began ringing. She got up and walked into the hallway and had a brief conversation and then hung up.

Bryan quickly took in the situation and came over. "What's going on?" he asked.

"We've identified the dead girl as Amanda Springer, age 19 from Philadelphia. She was working as a waitress and trying to become an actress."

"Cause of death?" asked Bryan.

"Blunt force trauma to the head."

"What else?" I asked.

"It seems she was a member of The Followers."

"How do you know that?" I asked.

"The parents told us that she had taken up with a religious group and had cut them off, according to the call I just got."

"Is there a problem?" asked Bryan reading her face.

"Richard said he didn't know the girl, but he was undercover with the Followers. He must have known her."

"I'm sure there's a simple explanation," I added not really sure if there was one or not.

"Hopefully, there is," she answered without conviction in her voice.

"Dinner is ready," announced Dustin. "We have black bean burgers, french fries, and salad. The buffet table is set, so help yourselves."

"Looks good," I said really meaning it this time. Dustin had outdone himself.

"Is that chocolate cake?" asked Buffy.

"That it is," replied Dustin smiling.

***

"As a courtesy," said Buffy Cunningham in her most professional voice, "I'm going to let you sit in on the interview with Richard. But remember you have no official standing here." Those words were aimed at me. Bryan as head of campus security needed no such instructions.

"I understand," I said. Good luck with that, I thought to myself.

The interview room was a standard bare room containing only a steel table and chairs. One wall had a mirror, which I assumed was a one way mirror, and up in the corner I noticed a camera. Richard was brought in and sat down. We all exchanged greetings and then Buffy got down to business. Clearly to me he looked tired, which wasn't surprising seeing that he just was released from the hospital.

"We've been unable to find Judy Johnson to help verify your story."

"What do you mean you can't find her?" asked Richard.

"She has disappeared, and there is no record of a Judy Johnson, so we're sure that wasn't her real name. We think she set you up. And we have no way to identify her."

"I have a picture of her," said Richard.

"You do?" asked Buffy surprised.

"Of course. I learned in military intelligence not to trust anyone. If you look at my phone you'll find a picture of her."

Buffy signaled to a police officer outside the room. He opened the door.

"Would you look through Mr. Hall's effects and bring us his cell phone?" The policeman nodded and soon returned with the phone. Buffy handed it to Richard. He played with the phone and then handed it to agent Cunningham.

"There are about five of them here," he said. "I took them without her knowing, just in case."

"Excellent. I'll have the FBI search using facial recognition."

Richard emailed them to the address that Buffy provided.

"The question is," said Bryan, "why was Richard set up and how did they know that he was working for the FBI?"

"That," said Buffy Cunningham with determination in her eyes, "is what I'm going to find out."

Chapter 8

B lake Carter had his camera aimed at me. I was sitting for a portrait to use on my book jacket and a few still shots for my modeling portfolio. This time I was dressed as Danny Black, or rather undressed as Danny Black.

"If Dustin hadn't told me you were a model, I never would have guessed, at least when you're dressed up as the professor. Clothes and glasses make a big difference."

"I'm not wearing any clothes," I said. I was posing with just a towel as if I had just stepped out of the shower and I was feeling slightly self-conscious.

"How about if you put that towel around your neck?" he suggested.

"I don't think so," I said as I pulled the towel closer around my waist.

"Let me take it, you don't have to use it if you don't want."

"Fine," I said and rolled up the towel and put it around my neck.

"Shit," Blake said as he held down the shutter button and I heard the continuous clicking. "You could make a lot of money with that shot."

"Is this what they call a money shot?" I asked.

"Not exactly, no."

"What is a money shot then?" I asked. He told me what the term meant. "We won't be doing that." I was slightly shocked.

"Now if you get dressed we'll take some stills for the book jacket. When is your next book coming out?" I walked across the room and began getting dressed.

"It's going to be released in February," I answered. "Crime stories seem to sell better in winter for some reason."

"Are you still planning to go to Provincetown?"

"I'm making a short visit next week and then a longer one next month."

"I'm really interested in doing a photo spread on the dig. I've run the idea by the editor of *History Today* and they are interested.

"With their millions of readers that would be good publicity for Cranmore College. I'll email you the travel details as soon as I have them."

"Great," he said as he picked up his camera. "Now sit on that stool and look pretty."

Richard Hall sat up at attention as agent Cunningham spoke. Bryan and I were with Richard at Dustin's apartment. Everyone thought it best that he not return to his apartment. Dustin was in the kitchen brewing up a pot of coffee.

"Thanks to you, Richard, we were able to get a hit on Judy Johnson. Your photos helped us identify her," Buffy Cunningham seemed to be in her element. "Her real name is Nancy Andrews. She has a record and is wanted for setting fire to a college library."

"Why would anyone want to set fire to a library?" I asked.

"The library was featuring a collection of anti-church literature. It was the target of fundamentalist church groups in the community. The burning of the library, we believe, was linked to some of the more extreme religious fanatics, but no one could ever prove it. Nancy Andrews was seen at the library just before the fire broke out and stood around in the crowd watching it burn. She was wanted for questioning, but disappeared. Now she's involved with the Followers and most likely is the one who set up Richard."

"But why?" asked Richard.

"Somehow, we believe, she suspected you of not being a true believer."

"And you believe that Cranmore College is somehow connected to all this?" I asked.

"We suspect that either students of Cranmore are members of the Followers, or that Cranmore is the target of their next protest, or possibly both."

"And what are we supposed to do?" asked Bryan.

"Keep your eyes open and look for anything out of the ordinary," she answered.

Big help! I thought to myself. Maybe I'll think of a plan.

"This one is heavy," said Madison as she held up another package from the Cape Cod dig.

"Let's have a look," I said as I took the package from her hands and placed it on the table. I took a letter opener and carefully split the tape holding the package closed. Tightly wrapped in bubble wrap and packed with styrofoam peanuts was a large bowl with a single handle.

It appeared to be made out of cheap porcelain with a white background and blue flowers.

"What a pretty soup tureen," exclaimed Madison as she picked it up and turned it around in her hand.

"It's a chamber pot," I said, "or as we call it in Maine, a piss pot."

"Yuck," she said and placed it back on the table.

"It beats running out to the privy in the back yard on a cold night. It's also from a much later date than the other artifacts, possibly early twentieth century."

"Really?"

"Which means there is more than one habitation of the site."

"That's not uncommon is it?"

"Not at all," I answered. "Parts of Cape Cod have been occupied for centuries. I'm even going to guess that there was once an Indian village on the site of the dig."

"Do you think that the archeologists will uncover Indian artifacts?"

"It's possible, but Native Americans were more or less nomadic and built few permanent dwellings. Smaller stone tools might be found."

"This is fascinating."

"One of our jobs will be to separate the different layers of history on the site."

"I can't wait to go."

"Provincetown," I said, "is going to be lots of fun and lots of work."

Walking across campus to meet Bryan at the cafeteria I spotted a pamphlet on the ground. I picked it up and headed over to the nearest trash can. As I was about to throw it away I noticed a simple cross on the front and under it the words "Change is coming."

Flipping open the pamphlet I saw that it was an invitation to a rally in a local park near the campus. "Come and be part of the change." I folded up the pamphlet and put it in my pocket.

"What's up?" asked Bryan as I took a seat at the table where he was waiting for me.

"I found this on the ground," I said and passed him the pamphlet. He picked it up and read through it.

"You think this is related to the Followers?"

"It's possible," I said. "That was my first thought."

"I think I'll go check it out."

"That's not a good idea," I said. "Someone will recognize you as campus security."

"I'll find someone to go then."

"Send me," I offered.

"You! You'll be spotted right away."

"This is one time when my professor drag is going to help. No one will recognize me without the glasses, the slicked-back hair, and the baggy clothing."

"If you unbutton your shirt everyone will be looking at your abs and not your face."

"Very funny," I said, but maybe it wasn't a bad idea. "Anyway the rally is after night fall, so there is less chance of being recognized."

"Okay, but just be careful. I wouldn't mention it to agent Cunningham until after the rally."

"Good idea," I agreed.

Norma Jean Baker was dressed in tan slacks and a bright blue smock with large red flowers and holding a hot curling iron over my head.

"You look very different with curly hair," she said as she continued to use the curling iron. "No one will recognize you for sure."

"I want to blend into the crowd," I said. I had told her about the rally. "Fortunately it will be dark."

"I'm going with you."

"I don't think that's a good idea."

"No one will recognize me. I'm going to dress up as one of those bag ladies that hangs out in the park and feeds pigeons. Maybe I'll meet some men, too. I sure could use a little romp in the bushes."

"No romping!" I said. "I don't want to have to bail you out of jail. Been there, done that."

"Buzz kill." She turned off the curling iron and unplugged the device. "There. Now you look like a… I don't know what. Let me go change and then we can go."

I looked into the mirror and saw a stranger looking back at me. Not bad looking but not much else either. I took Bryan's advice and unbuttoned my shirt. I wasn't sure even my friends would recognize me. Norma Jean came back into the room wearing a long cotton dressed that was worn and faded and carrying two shopping bags.

"What's in the bags?" I asked.

"Just old newspapers and rags."

"Okay, Norma Jean, let's go."

Chapter 9

I parked the car about two blocks from the park and Norma Jean and I proceeded on foot. When we arrived there appeared to be about fifty people of various ages gathered in one area. Milling around the edge of the area were the typical residents of the park. There were couples out for an evening stroll and a handful of what appeared to be the homeless. Norma Jean and I found a tree to stand under and observe the crowd from a safe distance.

Scanning the crowd of people I was relieved to see that I didn't recognize anyone as a Cranmore student. After a few minutes I spotted Buffy Cunningham. Her blonde hair was a dead giveaway. I imagined that she was undercover playing the dumb coed. The crowd grew as more young people arrived. I lost track of Buffy.

"Nice disguise," said a voice from behind me in the dark. I jumped. It was agent Cunningham.

"How did you see us?" I asked.

"I'm trained to look closely at people. Grandma here was a dead giveaway."

"Hey," said Norma Jean. "I'm not a grandma. I'm a vital woman in her prime."

"Sure you are," said Buffy rolling her eyes. "Stay out of the way. I have several agents here, and let me know if you observe anything unusual."

I looked out at the crowd and turned around and she was gone.

"How did she do that?" asked Norma Jean?

"She's Batman," I replied. "Or batty at the very least."

The crowd of young people seemed to tighten up and a young man and woman began to speak. At first it was difficult to hear, but as the crowd quieted down to listen, Norma Jean and I crept up closer.

"This country was founded as the Christian nation," said the woman. "We in this country have forgotten that."

"Apparently," I whispered to Norman Jean, "they've never read Thomas Paine, John Adams, or Thomas Jefferson."

"We have let the heathen hordes rule this country in their Godless ways," intoned the young man. "Now we must organized and fight back."

As the speech went on, about half the crowd drifted away. Those that remained moved closer to the speakers and applauded their words. Looking closer I recognized four of the listeners as students at Cranmore. I jotted down their names, though I was relieved to know they were not anthropology students.

The speeches droned on and I ceased to pay attention. All of a sudden I heard the word murder. "...and one of our followers, Amanda Springer was murdered. Murdered by those who would stop our movement. And I tell you that murder will not go unpunished." It was the woman who was speaking. Buffy Cunningham had worked her way to the front of the crowd and was nodding in agreement with the speakers."

"What's that silly bitch doing?" asked Norma Jean.

"Exercising her cover as a dumb blonde grad student. Notice how the male leader is looking at her."

"Notice the dirty looks she's getting from the female. I'm thinking she sees possible competition."

"How can you tell?" I asked.

"Women are always competing for male attention. She sees Buffy as a possible rival."

"I'm sure Buffy knows what she's doing," I said.

"Oh, yes," replied Norma Jean. "She knows exactly what she is doing."

The next morning I was up early and headed out to the college. I stopped by the cafeteria for coffee and a bagel. Buffy Cunningham seemed to appear out of nowhere.

"So what did you and grandma observe last night?" she asked as she sat down at my table with a cup of coffee.

"I saw four Cranmore students at the rally, only two of them stayed until the end." I passed her the notes I took last night.

"They're using Amanda Springer's murder to show that they are being persecuted."

"I noticed that. And they made a not-so-veiled threat. And I noticed you flirt with the leader and make the female leader jealous."

"They are the power couple of the group. We're checking them out now. They are Barbara and Joshua Levesque, though that probably isn't their real names. If I can drive a wedge between the two, then..." Two students I recognized were heading our way.

"And that's why I gave you a C on your paper, Ms. Cunningham." I said very loudly as two of my grad students strolled by. They looked at me and shook their heads in sympathy.

"Quick thinking," whispered Buffy.

"I need to get moving," I said as I started to get up. "See you later in class."

Madison was already at her desk going over student papers when I arrived. "You're starting early," I said as I headed to my desk.

"It's that intro class you gave me," she said. "They're a lot of work."

"That's because they are taking the course to fulfill one of the core requirements. They are not invested in the subject, but if we are lucky they might just decide to switch their majors."

"Does that ever happen?"

"Every year we get about five or six students who switch to anthropology."

"I guess I was one of them."

"I'm going to need you to cover my classes while I'm on the East Coast," I handed her a packet I had arranged. "Most of the material you are familiar with. My doctoral students will be working on their research, so you won't have to prepare class time."

"Good, I can use the extra time to work on my dissertation."

"At the end of this four week summer you will be Dr. Smith," I said. "And as it happens a position will be opening up on the faculty. The application is at the bottom of those papers I just gave you."

"Thank you Professor Littlefield."

"Please call me Luke."

"I don't know about that. Habits are hard to break."

"Just don't call me Danny."

Pottery and Poets

"I'd never do that. Danny Black is a bad ass."

Returning from my afternoon forensics class I saw a package on my desk that Madison must have left for me. The return address was from Higgins's dig on the cape. More pottery? I slowly opened the box.

"Buffy Cunningham is a jerk," snapped Madison as she came through the office door.

"Is she still acting up in class?"

"I get it that she's undercover, but she needs to tone it down. She is disruptive in class."

"I'll speak to her, but I have a feeling if she's still acting up in class, then there is someone in that class she's trying to impress with her bad ass attitude."

"That makes sense," sighed Madison. "I was beginning to take it personally. What's in the package?"

"I was just about to open it. More pottery most likely." I took the box cutter from my desk and slit open the tape holding the package together. The object was wrapped in layers of bubble wrap.

"It must be delicate china," said Madison as I began to carefully unwrap it. "That's more bubble wrap than they usually use."

"It's not pottery," I said as I took off the last layer of wrap and held it in my hand. "It's a human skull."

I was marinating steaks to grill later when Bryan came home with Richard Hall. Richard had been downgraded from suspect to person of interest. "Hi guys," I said as they came into the kitchen. "What's going on?"

"I'm not sure, but agent Cunningham wants to come over and meet with us. Something must be happening."

A few minutes later the door bell rang and Bryan went over to answer it and he returned with Buffy. I indicated that we all should sit down at the table. I offered everyone a glass of red wine and they all nodded.

"I know you are all wondering what's going on," she said as I passed her a wine glass.

"Good guess," I said. She shot me a look.

"Perhaps," said Bryan, "you could clarify a few points."

"Okay then," she said beginning the narrative. "Here's what we know so far. You, Richard, were working for us undercover trying to get information on the Followers. Your background in military intelligence made you useful for us. You made some initial contacts with several members, one of them being Judy Johnson, also known as Nancy Andrews. She came to you saying that she wanted out of the cult because they were going to do something dramatic. You took her to a motel to be safe. Is that it so far?"

"Yes," agreed Richard.

"Very good," she continued. "But you had no idea what that big thing was going to be?"

"No, she never said. I got the feeling she didn't know."

"Then you go out to get some groceries and when you got back Judy was gone and that a dead girl whom you had never seen was in the motel room."

Richard nodded.

"It became clear to us that you were set up from the very beginning. Judy Johnson set you up for the murder of that girl. Whose idea was it to choose that motel?"

"It was Judy. She said that she knew of a safe motel where everyone minded their own business."

"So it was her idea to go to that particular motel?"

"Yes, it was." Richard was looking puzzled at this line of questioning.

Buffy reached into her handbag and brought out two photos. "Have you seen these two individuals before?"

"Yes," said Richard as he pointed to the photograph of the man. "He's the desk clerk at the motel, and I've seen her cleaning rooms."

I picked up the photographs. "These are the speakers at last night's rally." I passed them back to Buffy.

"That's right," said Buffy. "Barbara and Joshua Levesque. Barbara seems to be the weaker link. So tonight I have a date with Joshua and I have every intention of making sure Barbara finds out about it. And Professor Littlefield I have a part for you to play, if you are interested."

We all listened as she told us the plan.

Chapter 10

Madison held the skull in one hand and a magnifying glass in the other. "What do you notice about the skull?" I asked.

"The cranial ridge indicates male as does the shape and size of the mandible. Nasal cavity and eye sockets suggest Caucasian."

"Age?"

"Adult by the fused cranial plates."

"And age of remains?"

"Teeth are in good condition but worn. No dental work in evidence, so I would say this individual lived before the 1850s."

"The skull is in good condition, but notice the leaching of minerals. I would place this individual as much earlier, possibly late 1600s."

"But it's so well preserved."

"It's Cape Cod. It was buried in sand, which has preserved the skull remarkably well. Remember that it was found at an excavation with early colonial artifacts. We must look at the context of the site as well as the condition of the skull."

"Yes, of course," agreed Madison. "What else can we learn?"

"Professor Higgins sent along a report and photos of the find. That may help, but I'm sending this over to the lab for chemical analysis."

"What do you think they will find?"

"We shouldn't speculate without evidence," I said using the professional answer.

"But?"

"I would guess they will find high levels of lead. The use of lead glazed pottery and pewter, which in colonial times was an amalgam of tin and lead was common among the wealthier classes."

"Just the wealthy?"

"Servants and the poorer classes used wooden utensils, unglazed pottery and vessels made of horn. They couldn't afford pewter and glazed pots."

"Lucky for them."

"I don't think anyone was really lucky back then. Sixty percent of the colonists to the New World died within the first year. Most would be lucky to live past forty."

I looked up at the clock on the wall. It was time to get started. "I have to go," I said. "You are in charge of my classes for the next week."

Buffy Cunningham picked me up at the house and drove me to the airport to pick up a rental car. I had shed my professor clothing and was dressed in tight jeans and a white shirt that was cut tight as well.

"Explain the plan to me again," I said.

"You are going to check into the Sky View Motel and take notes of what's going on."

"And you're not using a regular FBI agent why?"

"Because experienced criminals are often able to identify someone who isn't quite right. I don't know what it is, but it's like a sixth sense."

"I'm not buying that," I said.

"Okay, we don't have anyone quite as good looking as you. You are distracting to say the least. People who look at you won't be thinking about spies and agents."

"You're pimping me out?"

"Maybe Mrs. Levesque will like what she sees."

"So you're flirting with the husband and I'm supposed to flirt with the wife?"

"You make it sound so contrived," she said laughing.

"And the rental car?"

"You're supposed to be in town for business. The rental car will be a good supporting detail."

"I'm not sure exactly what I'm supposed to do."

"Play it by ear. Take this cell phone," she said as she passed me one of the latest models. "It's got a tracking device in it and a listening device as well."

"Someone will be listening?"

"Yes, they will. You might not want to take it into the bathroom with you."

"Good point," I said. I got out of the car and walked over to the car rental company. I picked out the most expensive car on the lot.

Barbara Levesque was at the desk of the Sky View Motel when I checked in. I was wearing cargo shorts, a button-down shirt that was unbuttoned, and a pair of dark glasses. Barbara's eyes were on me the moment I walked into the motel office.

"Good afternoon," I said. "Do you have a room available?" I took off my glasses and looked into her eyes.

"I believe we do," she said as I saw her eyes scan over me. I wasn't used to flirting with women so I was somewhat at a loss as to what to do next.

"I've just flown in from Maine for a business conference and I don't know anyone here."

"I'd be happy to help you with anything," she said. The way she said "anything" lead me to believe that she wasn't talking about directions to the nearest pizza joint. Maybe this was going to be easier than I thought.

"Room thirty-two," she said as she handed me the keys.

"Thanks," I said. "Maybe I'll see you around later."

"Count on it," she said.

"Smooth," said Buffy Cunningham to me over the phone. She had been listening in on my registering for the room. "You need to work on your game. The woman was practically throwing herself at you."

"How can you tell?" I asked.

"Just pretend she's a good looking young guy."

"Why young?"

"You're hopeless," she sighed. "Anyway, I have a date with the husband tonight. Try to make some time with the wife will you?"

"I'll try," I said. I could swear she muttered "asshole" over the phone.

I woke up after a short nap and headed over to the office. Barbara Levesque was working the front desk still.

"Is there a good restaurant around here?" I asked.

"I was just about to fix something for dinner. Why don't you join me?"

"Will your husband be joining us?" I asked pointing to her ring.

"He's away for the evening," she said. "He won't be back until much later."

"Thank you," I said putting on my best fake smile. "I don't like to eat alone."

I was just about to try and say something flirty when my cell phone rang. I picked it up. It was Buffy.

"Hello," I said.

"Is Barbara Levesque with you now?"

"Yes."

"The police are on their way over there. You need to get out of there. Meet me at the park as soon as you can."

"On my way," I said and hung up. "Sorry, but I have to meet a business acquaintance. Rain check?"

"Sure," she said. "Anytime."

I left the office and headed to my car. Two police cars pulled up to the motel as I left the parking lot.

I parked the rental car near the park where I recognized Buffy's car. I noticed that her windows were open. I guess the FBI didn't worry about locking up their cars. I spotted police cars and flashing lights. Buffy came up to me as I got out of the car.

"What's going on?" I asked.

"Joshua Levesque was found murdered in the park. The police are on their way to inform the wife. Do you know if she was there all afternoon?"

"As far as I know she was working the motel desk all afternoon."

"Well," she said, "our number one murder suspect has been murdered and our number two suspect has an alibi."

"Now what?" I asked.

"Now we wait for the other shoe to drop."

"I think we should take a look at the body."

"It's a crime scene. Police only."

"I'm a professional anthropologist in case you've forgotten."

"I guess it wouldn't hurt," she sighed, but didn't look happy.

We headed over to the area that was cordoned off by yellow crime scene tape. The police had erected portable barriers around the body to keep the gory details from the crowd that was gathering in the park. Something about sirens and flashing emergency lights draws the public, like insects to a light bulb. Buffy and I stepped around the barriers. Joshua Levesque was lying face down on the ground with his head covered with blood.

"That's odd," I said looking at the body.

"What's odd?" asked Buffy.

"He's dressed up, but no shoes. He's barefoot." I knelt down and took a closer look at the body. "And his feet are cut up. Like he ran over broken glass."

"Don't touch anything," yelled a woman's voice. I stood up. "I'm the medical examiner." She was all of five feet tall and had dark hair bound back by a strip of rawhide. I placed her age at mid-thirties. She was sporting a simple wedding band. I figured that was all she could wear and still pull on rubber gloves for her job.

"Dr. Luke Littlefield," I said holding out my hand. "Anthropology professor at Cranmore College." Her eyes did a quick scan and then she smiled and took my hand.

"I've actually heard of you, Dr. Littlefield. "I'm Mary Brooks."

"This is Buffy Cunningham of the FBI," I said remembering my manners.

"Perhaps," said Buffy getting to the point, "you could give us a preliminary report."

"I'll have to examine the victim in the lab to give a full report, but let me take a look." She bent down to examine the body. "Blunt force trauma to the head."

"You might want to take a look at the jacket," I said. "From the angle I'm looking at the body there seems to be something under the fold of the jacket."

"It looks like a bullet hole," she said. "I'm not sure which one was the cause of death yet."

"I noticed his feet," I said. Dr. Brooks took a look at the feet.

"The feet are cut up," she said.

"I didn't see any broken glass on the ground," I said pointing to the walkway where people were standing behind the police line.

"We need to let the medical examiner do her job," said Buffy grabbing me by the arm. "Why don't you go home?"

"Are you wearing body glitter?" I asked. The streetlight had caused me to see the small colorful reflections. "I didn't know that was FBI issue."

"Funny guy," she replied. "Some idiot was tossing glitter on everyone out on the street. I think I'll track him down and see what he knows."

"Makes you look almost human," I said and took off for home before she could reply.

Chapter 11

It was time to leave for Cape Cod in Massachusetts, and I was happy to leave behind murders and FBI agents. Bryan dropped me off at LAX where I was to wait for a flight to Boston. It was early morning and the airport was busy. I checked my bags, made it through airport security, and sat at the gate to wait for the flight. I was in luck and the flight was on time. I watched the jet pull up and the passengers get off. It must have been a long flight by the stressed look on the faces of the passengers. I watched as the flight crew deplaned and a new flight crew boarded. Out the window I could see the maintenance workers getting the jet ready.

Passengers were already lining up at the gate, which made no sense to me as all seats were assigned and everyone would be called by rows. By the time my row was called half the plane was full and the overhead bins were overflowing with carryon luggage. I only brought a small bag with a few snacks and my eBook reader.

The in-flight entertainment consisted of small TV sets placed in the back of the seats. I chose to read and ignore the commercial television programs playing on the screens. I arrived in Boston after the six hour flight and headed to the car rental agency.

Traffic was heavy as I headed south of the city, but nowhere near as bad as the LA freeways at rush hour. Provincetown is not far from Boston as the crow flies, but the forty-seven mile drive takes close to two hours because of the single lane roads and the local traffic. Once you cross over the Sagamore Bridge that spans the Cape Cod Canal you know you are on the cape.

As I hit the town of Truro I was surrounded by sand dunes that seem to creep up to the road. Off in the distance I could see the Pilgrim monument that towers over Provincetown.

I pulled into the small parking lot of the Light Keepers Bed and Breakfast. It was a compound of three New England houses that were connected on the second floor by wooden walkways. On the roof of the larger house was a sundeck and all the windows had window boxes filled with red geraniums.

"Welcome," said the blond middle-aged man as I walked into the lobby. "You must be Dr. Littlefield. I'm Bruce Wilson the host. We've been expecting you. David, our guest is here."

"Hello," said another tall good looking man of middle age. "I'm David Preston. Let me show you to your room."

"How did you know it was me?" I asked.

"We googled you, though you are much better looking than your college photo. We've put you on the first floor in the back. We serve breakfast in the lobby and the roof deck is open. We have a fenced in back yard with a hot tub and it's clothing optional."

He led me down a short corridor and opened the door. The room was large with windows that looked out over the garden. It was nicely furnished with Victorian antiques and there was a small private bath.

"Is there anything we can do for you?" asked David.

"It's been a long trip; I think I want to take a nap."

"Let us know if there is anything you need."

"Thanks," I said. I sat my suitcase down and took out my phone to call Bryan and tell him I was safe and sound.

"Hey handsome, are you settled in?" asked Bryan when he picked up the call.

"I'm just about to catch some sleep. Anything new there?" I asked.

"Richard and Dustin are going away for a few days. They said they need to regroup after what happened."

"I don't blame them. I'm surprised they haven't had a meltdown yet. Richard goes missing and then finds a dead body."

"I think it was probably harder on Dustin. Richard is ex-military and probably has seen much worse. What are your plans?"

"After my nap I'll unpack and go grab some dinner. Then tomorrow I'll meet with Higgins and his team at the dig. Hopefully I can get some research done as well and then I'm heading home."

"I can't wait to go there with you. Oh, by the way Buffy Cunningham said that the autopsies were completed on both murder victims."

"Any addition information?"

"None that she mentioned."

"Hey, do you think you could get your buddies at headquarters to give you a copy of the autopsies?"

"Probably. Why?" Bryan asked puzzled.

"Email me the copies if you can. I'm just curious. Maybe I can use them in a class sometime."

"Sure thing. Enjoy your time away. I love you, you know."

"Back at you big guy. I'll call you later."

"Stay safe," said Bryan and then hung up the phone. I opened the windows, closed the drapes and stripped off my clothes and crawled into bed. In a few minutes I was sound asleep.

It was late evening when I woke from the nap and I was hungry. I took a shower and got dressed and headed down to Commercial Street. The day trippers had gone home and the night people were out in force. A drag queen was on one of the street corners passing out flyers to the drag show. Everywhere I looked men were holding hands with men and women with women. It was a festive atmosphere.

I had been to Provincetown several times and knew my way around. Like many popular summer destinations, the names of businesses had changed over the years, but everything else remained pretty much untouched.

The Lobster Pot Restaurant was one of those places that had been there for years. I headed upstairs to the bar and grabbed a stool near the window.

"Good evening," said the bar tender whose name tag declared her to be Betty. "What can I get you?"

"A nice iced cosmopolitan would be great."

"Coming right up. Would you like a menu?"

"Yes, please."

Betty placed a menu in front of me and I looked it over. There really was only one choice for this transplanted Maine boy, and I ordered the lobster dinner.

"Here on vacation?" asked a voice sitting next to me. I looked over to see a dark haired, good looking gentleman in his late thirties.

"Actually here on business. I'm an anthropologist. Are you vacationing?" I asked.

"Actually I live here. James Cameron."

"Luke Littlefield. Your name sounds familiar." I had heard the name before, but couldn't recall where."

"I'm a writer," he said.

"You're a poet," I said recalling the name. I had read some of his published poems that had appeared in several literary journals in the college library.

"I didn't think anyone read those," he said smiling at me. "I make most of my living writing gay fiction."

"Like *Western Justice*? I've read it. I've published a few books too under the name of Danny Black. Mostly I write crime novels."

"Danny Black? The model?"

"How do you know about that?"

"Anyone who reads your books knows you're a model, too. I didn't know you were an anthropologist as well. That's even more interesting."

"I try to keep my professional life separate from my other work. I'm not sure the academic community would take a male model anthropologist seriously."

Just then my dinner arrived. The lobster was too hot to crack open, so I grabbed a clam, opened the shell, took out the clam, removed the membrane, washed it in salt water and dipped it in butter. The process was long, but the taste was worth the effort.

Betty brought another lobster dinner and placed it in front of James. We ate dinner in silence, except for the sound of cracking lobster shells.

"I think I'll go over to the Boatslip for a drink," said James when we had finished our dinner and the shells had been cleared away. "Care to come along?"

"Sure," I said. "I'm wide awake because I'm still on West Coast time."

The Boatslip is famous for its afternoon tea dance, but it's the "go to" place in the evening also. Hotel rooms surround a huge open deck in Provincetown Harbor. It was Bear Week and men of generous size were partying on the balconies and frolicking in the pool. The dance floor was crowded with shirtless men dancing to the DJ and the bars were overflowing. James and I did manage to find a relatively quiet spot for a beer.

"And what is an anthropologist doing in Provincetown?" asked James after his first gulp of beer.

"The archeology team of Cranmore College is doing an historical dig just outside of town. They're uncovering artifacts and cataloging them. My job will be to look at the whole and reconstruct daily life based on their findings. There are various strata so I'll have to determine which artifacts belong to which time period."

"Won't that be evident by the placement of the layers?"

"In theory, yes. But some of the oldest artifacts could have been used by later inhabitants. It was not unusual for some objects to be passed down through the generations. And then there's the problem of those artifacts that are found on the border line of the next layer. Do they belong to the earlier layer or the later layer. It's not an exact science."

"It sounds like interesting work."

"It is, but what about you?"

"Nothing much to tell. I worked for a government agency for ten years and then I published my first work of fiction. Then I got bold and wrote a few poems."

"Which agency did you work for?"

"The FBI. The job got to me after a while. I'll bet you've never met and agent before. Most people go their whole lives and never see one of us."

"I've met an agent before, and I have to tell you it wasn't the highlight of my day." I went on and told him about Buffy Cunningham and two murders.

"Wow! Sounds like a real mess and she sounds like a real bitch."

"I don't disagree."

"I suppose a great guy like you is in a relationship?" he asked abruptly.

"As a matter of fact I am. To a great guy who's built like the proverbial brick shit house."

"And you?"

"I was but he died."

"Sorry to hear that," I said. What do you say to that?

"It's been rough."

"I'm buying another round of beers, so drink up."

Chapter 12

It was late morning when I woke up, not yet acclimated to the east coast time zone. I threw on some shorts and a tee shirt, and I headed to the breakfast room where Bruce and David were serving a large breakfast. I had a nice cheese omelet with wheat toast and a rather large cup of coffee.

"You're causing quite a stir among the guests," said David refilling my coffee.

"Why?" I asked.

"Do you own a mirror?" remarked Bruce as he passed by. That reminded me that I needed to dress up in professor drag to go out to the dig. I looked around the dining room. It was filled with good looking, in-shape middle aged men. Where were they when I was single?

I went back to my room and changed into my loose clothing and thick-framed glasses, and then slicked back my hair. I checked myself in the mirror and was convinced that I wouldn't be getting any second looks now. Just as I was about to leave my cell phone went off. I looked at the caller ID.

"Good morning, Madison. It's rather early in California isn't it?"

"It's 7:00 am here and I'm at the office getting ready for class. The reason I called is to tell you that we just got another package from the dig. This time the package contains bones, and I think we might have a whole skeleton. I was hoping you'd know seeing as you're there."

"I haven't met the team yet, I was just on my way to see Professor Higgins and his interns. I'll ask about the skeleton. In the mean time you can catalogue the findings when you get a chance. How are the classes going?"

"Not bad at all. I'm rather excited to tell the truth."

"You'll make a great instructor. I've got to get over there now so good luck with the classes." I rang off and headed out to my car. I wasn't exactly sure where the dig was, so I put in the coordinates into my GPS unit.

The female GPS voice seemed to be taking on a nagging attitude as I followed directions. Of course that could have just been my imagination. I found the one lane road and followed it down to where the dig was taking place. A huge canvas canopy was covering the area where about five grad students were digging. Bert Higgins was easy to pick out because of his flaming red hair. However his hair wasn't the only aspect of him that was flaming. Today he was wearing cargo shorts and a pith helmet like a Victorian explorer.

"Well, if it isn't the dishy queen of anthropology come for a visit," he said and gave me a hug.

"Good to see you, Bert," I said and didn't really mean it. "My teaching assistant said you had sent more bones over to us."

"Yes, we think we have a complete skeleton. Come take a look." Bert led me to the area of the dig. It was neatly cut soil and it looked like they had uncovered four distinct layers.

"Where did you find the bones?" I asked.

"Not here, but down there," he said pointing, "about one hundred yards away. This site here seems to be a dump site."

"What made you want to dig over there?"

"There was a pile of stones that didn't seem to be placed there by any natural means. It seemed to be some type of cairn. We figured they were placed there. We only had to dig down about three feet and we found the skull and later the bones."

"Only one individual?"

"Yes, so it wasn't a grave yard, but only a grave."

"Did you get the reports I sent you on the artifacts?" I asked.

"Yes, you confirmed what we suspected. It was good to have another set of eyes on them. Once we finish here we hope you can write up a good narrative of the site."

"I'll do my best. I'll be back in three weeks and set up shop. Now show me what else you've found."

My muscles ached from bending down and examining layers of the dig, so when I got back to my room I changed into swim briefs and headed to the hot tub. There were already four guys in the tub when I lowered myself into the hot water. It took me a few minutes to realize that I was the only one wearing swim wear. I remembered that the backyard was clothing optional.

"I'm Joe and this is Pete," said Joe who was sitting next to me. Pete was on his left. That's Bill and Fred," said Joe indicating the guys who were in the water opposite me.

"I'm Luke," I said.

"Where are you from?" asked the guy named Bill.

"West Hollywood."

"You look familiar," said Pete. *The Benson and Bloom Catalogue* had many gay subscribers. In fact if I had to guess I'd say that gay men made up most of the customers. Was it possible they recognized me from the catalog?

"We're going over to the Atlantic House for drinks later if you'd like to come along."

"Why not," I responded. Suddenly all four got up and I was eye level with four penises of various shapes and sizes.

"See you around eight thirty," said Bill and the four of them trotted off.

The afternoon was sunny and warm and I spent most of it in a lawn chair in the yard going over the findings and reports that Bert Higgins's group had gathered. Slowly patterns were emerging that would help me with the narrative I was charged with preparing. Bert told me that the Provincetown Historical Society wanted to make it an historical site with signs and displays. I tried to not become distracted by the clothing optional atmosphere in the guest house's backyard, but it was different.

I had worked through lunch and was getting very hungry, so I set off for Commercial Street to find something to eat. It wasn't yet the height of the tourist season, but the town was still filled with tourists of every type. I love to watch the straight couples as they gawk at the colorful street theater that is Provincetown. The wives cling to their husbands as if we might snatch them away. And there were a few of them that I suspected wouldn't mind being snatched away.

I found a nice restaurant near the water that had a back deck for dining. I was led to a table and ordered a glass of white wine. The view was awesome and I made a mental note to come back with Bryan.

After my meal of baked haddock, I headed back up to my room to take a nap before going out with the boys. I tried to call Bryan but the call went to voice mail, so I left a brief message and turned in.

It was eight thirty in the evening when there was a knock at the door and the four boys came to take me to the Atlantic House, known by everyone as the A House. It is one of the oldest bars in the country and opened first in 1798. It was the preferred watering hole to such luminaries as Tennessee Williams and Eugene O'Neill. The four boys, I learned were all friends from New York City who preferred Provincetown to Fire Island. Pete was a lawyer, Bill was an accountant, Joe was a social worker, and Fred was some type of computer wizard. The bar was crowded and we grabbed a beer and found a small table to gather around.

It was clear that my four new friends were looking for dates. The bar was noisy and when my cell phone went off I hurried outside to take the call.

"Bryan, good to hear your voice," I said.

"Yours too. Sorry I missed your call, but we had a situation on campus."

"A situation?"

"Yes, we had a demonstration by the Followers on campus. They had signs saying things like 'unbelievers must perish,'" and 'Cranmore needs to be purified.'"

"They're just a group of nut jobs," I said.

"It got ugly. About a hundred Cranmore students made a counter-demonstration. I had to call the local police to help my guys break it up."

"Sounds like you earned your money today."

"And then some. Can't wait for you to come home."

"I'll be on the morning flight tomorrow. I can't wait to come back here with you."

"By the way. The autopsy reports are on my desk. I didn't have time to email them to you."

"Just keep them. I'll be home tomorrow and I have plenty of work to do on the plane."

I hung up the phone and looked at my watch. If I was going to get on a plane tomorrow I had best get back and get some sleep. I had arranged to take a small prop job to Boston to catch my flight, saving me a few hours of driving time.

Walking down colorful Commercial Street I was startled when a voice called out: "Danny Black!" I quickly scanned the area and spotted James Cameron seated at an outside cafe table with two other men.

"Danny," he said. "Come and meet my friends." I walked over to the group. "This is Buford Chase, and Lawrence Stafford."

"I know those names," I said stunned. Chase was a national reporter who wrote articles for major magazines and Stafford was a *New York Times* bestselling author of suspense novels. We shook hands all around.

"Danny Black is his *nom-de-plume*. His real name is Luke Littlefield and he's an anthropology professor in West Hollywood," explained James.

"That sounds more interesting," said Buford. He was somewhere in his forties and remarkably good looking, but didn't look a thing like the photograph on his book jacket.

"I read that you are a model, too," said Lawrence. "Looking at you I believe it." Lawrence was late thirties and had a head of frizzy red hair.

"I'm shocked that you know who I am at all," I said.

"Crime novels based on actual cases," said James, "are always entertaining and much more bizarre than straight fiction."

"Your last book," added Buford, "the one about serial killer Mike Perkins, was one of the most chilling things I've read."

"Luke is working here on the dig that's happening out on Shaggy Road. Have a seat Luke," James pointed to an empty chair. "We call ourselves the Provincetown Poets."

"How long will you be here in Provincetown?" asked Lawrence.

"I'm flying back to California tomorrow. Then I'll be back for a month or so at the end of the early summer term."

"You'll have to join our little group," suggested Buford. "We can always use new blood."

"I'd like that," I said. "I don't have any writer friends."

"You do now," said James and the other two nodded in agreement.

Chapter 13

Traveling coast to coast is like time travel. I gained extra hours on the flight back to California. Looking at the California scenery I realized how much I felt at home in New England with its lush green foliage and lakes and ponds. Bryan picked me up at the airport, and I went directly to my office. The semester was winding down, and I needed to make sure everything was going smoothly.

"Professor Littlefield," exclaimed Madison when I entered the office. "I didn't expect you back until tomorrow."

"I felt guilty leaving you with all the work, and I wanted to see if you needed any help."

"The classes are going well. Finals are in two weeks and I'm trying to cover everything before the end of the semester."

"You need to work on your dissertation," I reminded her.

"I've an appointment to defend it next week. Would you sit in?"

"Of course," I said. I knew her thesis was solid and was backed up by original research. She would pass, no doubt about it. "I am the department head after all."

"You must have a lot of department work for the end of the academic year."

"I do indeed," I said and I picked up the pile of papers on my desk and got to work.

Bryan had dinner ready when I got home. It was a good thing because I was exhausted from the flight and my late afternoon at the office. He had grilled a couple of steaks and baked some potatoes.

"Dustin and Norma Jean would have a fit," I said as I dug into the meal.

"I admire vegetarians, but I love a good steak. So how was your time on the cape?"

"I got to see the dig site and talk to Bert Higgins. He clarified my job, so I'll need to get busy as soon as the summer session is over. I also made some new friends." I told him about the Provincetown poets.

"Were they hot?" asked Bryan and I detected a little jealousy.

"Nowhere in the same class with you, and you know you have nothing to worry about."

"I know, but I do like confirmation once in a while."

"I'll give you some confirmation as soon as dinner is over."

"That's what I was hoping for."

Madison and I were in the lab placing the bones from the Provincetown dig on the light table trying to piece together a whole skeleton. This was not going to be as easy as I originally thought.

"I'm having trouble identifying this bone," said Madison as she held it under a magnifying glass. I stepped over beside her and picked up the bone.

"I'm not surprised," I said. "It's not a human bone."

"You think he was buried with animals?" she asked.

"Probably not. It most likely is from a later time."

"And look at this," Madison pointed to two long bones on the table. "We have almost a whole skeleton."

"Notice that it's in pretty good condition. Now I need you to see if these bones are consistent with the characteristics of the skull."

"Age and sex? Ethnicity?"

"All of the above," I said and then thought about it. I was treating her as if she was still an undergraduate. "Sorry, I forget that you are almost a PhD."

"No problem. You're keeping me on my toes. Bone color and condition of the bones is consistent with that of the skull. Sex and age appear to be the same, pending microscopic examination."

"Excellent."

"Will we need to send out for a DNA test?"

"Not needed." I said. "Single grave of a European male prior to 1700 is pretty conclusive. I'm going to leave it up to you to write up the final report."

"Thank you," she said and smiled.

I left Madison to continue her work and headed over to Bryan's office. A new security officer was working the main desk.

"May I help you?" he asked. I had the feeling that he didn't know I was a professor.

"I'm here to see Chief Sullivan.

"The chief is busy," he said in an officious tone. "Can I give him a message?"

"Yes, tell him his gay lover is here for his office booty call." The new recruit visibly paled and went into Bryan's office. He came out with his face burning.

"Go right in Professor Littlefield."

"New recruit?" I asked as I took a seat by Bryan's desk.

"Sorry about that. Yes, and I gave him an earful."

"You have the autopsies?"

"Here they are. Not much to say about them," he said as he passed them to me.

I studied them for a while. "Both were killed with a single shot, same weapon. No evidence of a struggle. Levesque had sex shortly before death and his feet were cut and had glass shards embedded in his feet." And then one more item caught my eye. "Can I keep these?"

"If you want, why?"

"Just working on a theory," I answered.

Buffy Cunningham had toned down her dumb blonde act in my intro class. I was taking back the class for the summer session review to give Madison time to finalize her dissertation. If all went well she would be Madison Smith PhD and I could hire her as an instructor for the fall term.

"Why are you back?" asked Buffy as she opened her notebook. "Where's the Madison chick?"

"Ms. Smith," I said with emphasis, "has other things to do. Is there a problem Miss Cunningham?" I gave her a look that seemed to stop her in her tracks.

"No," she said. "No problem."

"Good. Now let's review the case study on page 634 of your text book." The class was busy taking notes and the time went by quickly. I returned to my office to look over the class schedules for the fall semester.

"Am I interrupting?" asked Buffy as she entered my office.

"Agent Cunningham, what can I do for you?"

"I just wanted to give you an update."

"Please do. I wasn't here to see the demonstration. And I'm not clear as to how any of this fits together."

"Let me start at the beginning. The FBI has been following this group called the Followers for the past year. We have information that they are a terrorist group working as Christian zealots. They believe in a new world order where religious laws will replace civil law."

"Yes, I understand that. We also have people who believe they've been abducted by aliens. Being crazy isn't a crime."

"We had credible information that they were going to blow up a public building as the first step. Since they seemed to have settled in this area, we believe Cranmore College was in danger."

"Good God!"

"So we moved in. Richard Hall seemed to be perfectly situated to infiltrate the group. He has military training and is here as a grad student."

"This part I know. What I don't understand is how everything went wrong."

"Good point. Let me share my theory."

"Let's go somewhere for coffee so we can talk," I suggested. "There's a little coffee shop about a block from here."

"Lead the way."

We ordered our coffee and found a small table in the corner of the coffee shop. It wasn't a busy time of day and there were only a few business people there with their laptops out.

"Does Richard ever come here?" asked Buffy.

"Yes, he does as a matter of fact, but that's an odd question to ask."

"Look around and tell me what you see."

"I see a few grad students working on their laptops and some business people checking their smart phones." And then it hit me like a ton of bricks. "If Richard checked his email from here..."

"Then," said Buffy taking up the narrative, "someone could have hacked his laptop because this is an open network."

"But doesn't the FBI encrypt messages?"

"Yes, but anyone looking at his email would see the encryption. They wouldn't necessarily know that it was the FBI, but they would be suspicious of anything out of the ordinary."

"I see."

"The Followers seem to be a very savvy group. Any newcomers are researched and Richard's emails raised some red flags. They set him up."

"That's a rather extreme measure to take isn't it? Why not just drop him from the group?"

"Because he might be able to recognize someone. What better way than to set him up for murder? He would be totally discredited. This is an extremist group we're dealing with."

"One thing bothers me," I said looking at her.

"What's that?"

"I read the autopsy reports of both victims. There were traces of copolymer aluminized plastic on both bodies."

"What?"

"Body glitter."

"So?"

"So you had body glitter on you the other night. I asked you about it and you said that someone was throwing glitter around on the street."

"You're right," she said and shot out of her chair. "I need to check this out."

And she was gone.

Chapter 14

It was a pleasant evening, and Bryan and I were sitting out on the porch enjoying a beer. It was one of those evenings when we had no plans and nowhere to be. Bryan was only wearing shorts and flip flops and I was finding it distracting.

"What was in that large envelope that came in the mail?" asked Bryan.

"I think it's the photos that Blake took for my portfolio."

"You didn't look at them?"

"No, I didn't. Feel free to take a look if you like." Bryan shot out of his chair and went into the house and came back with the package. He carefully opened it and began looking at the photos. There were about twenty of them.

"These are really good," he said as he went through them. "Blake is a talented photographer. What the …?" He held up the last one.

"I forgot about that one," I said. It was the photo of me with nothing but a towel around my neck.

"That's hot. We ought to leak it on the internet. Your books would sell for sure."

"I don't think it would do much for my teaching career."

"You've got tenure, don't forget."

"I made the photo for a lark. Now put it away. Here comes Norma Jean." She had pulled up in her red mustang and made her way to the porch.

"I need a beer," she said as she sat down in one of the chairs.

"I'll get it," said Bryan as he headed for the kitchen. He returned and placed the beer in her hand. She took a long swallow before she spoke.

"I think I killed a man," she said finally.

"What do you mean you killed a man?" demanded Bryan.

"Who did you kill?" I asked.

"Jenks Carter, the man I've been seeing."

"You better explain," said Bryan. Norman Jean had been known to dramatize a time or two.

"Jenks and I were fooling around," she said finally. "And then he grabbed his chest in pain. I called 911 and they took him away."

"Do you know where they took him?" I asked. She nodded her head.

"Then we better go and find out," I said as I went into the house to get my keys. We were all silent on the drive to the hospital.

The emergency room was crowded and we had to wait in line at the desk to talk to the nurse.

"We're looking for Jenks Carter," said Bryan. "He was brought in about two hours ago."

"Let me see," said the nurse as she hit some keys on her computer. "He's in room 617."

"Thank you," said Bryan as he waved us over. "Let's go."

It was apparent that Bryan knew his way around the hospital, and then I remembered that as a cop he had probably been here many times. Norma Jean ran into the room.

"Babe," said Jenks from his hospital bed. "Sorry to give you a scare."

"What the hell happened?" asked Norma Jean. She was visibly pale.

"Gall bladder attack. I'm having surgery tomorrow. Who are your friends?"

Norma Jean introduced us and we shook hands. Jenks, though elderly, seemed to be in robust health.

"Nice to meet you both. Norma Jean has told me all about you."

"Don't believe a word of it," I said.

"She lies," added Bryan.

"See what assholes I have around me," replied Norma Jean finally smiling.

"She's lucky to have you. I have two sons and I'm lucky if I get one call a month."

"We should let you rest," said Bryan, "before the nurse comes in and shoos us away."

"I'll be in to check up on you," said Norma Jean as she went over and kissed him.

"He seems nice," I said when we got into the car.

"Not your usual loser," said Bryan.

"Is it serious?" I asked her.

"I think he's the one," she replied and then started to cry.

It was Saturday morning and Bryan's antique shop was filled with bargain hunters. Bryan was busy in the backroom cleaning up some furniture he had just acquired at an estate sale. I came in to check on Norma Jean. I was worried about her. She wasn't one for tears and her breakdown in my car unsettled me.

"How are you doing?" I asked her when I entered the shop.

"Much better. Sorry about the tears thing. I was really tired and I thought it was my fault. After all, men seem to die when I get close to them." The gentleman she met at the Maine project had been murdered.

"Not your fault. People die for a variety of reasons. Anyway I've come to take your place here so you can go to the hospital. You'll want to be there while Jenks is in surgery.

"Those nurse bitches only let me visit for an hour at a time."

"They're just following doctors' orders."

"I've done a couple of doctors in my time. They're not as good in the sack as you'd think."

"Good to know," I said rolling my eyes.

"You'd think they'd know how to please a woman, having studied the body and all."

"Anyway," I said to change the subject. The old Norma Jean was back, "I'll take over here and you can go to the hospital. Give Jenks my best."

"I will, thanks for taking over. I'll be back after lunch." I watched her drive away in her red mustang.

"Can you grab the other end?" asked Bryan as he stood behind a large Victorian desk.

"Where do you want it?"

"Over there by that dining table."

"What did you think of Norma Jean?"

"She seems fine this morning. And by fine I mean crazy."

"How many of those posters have you sold?" I asked pointing to the image of myself on cardboard.

"Two this week."

"We could make up one of you. You are model worthy."

"Thanks, but I don't photograph well." Bryan is extremely handsome, well built, and a real hunk, but he was right. As hot looking as he is, he doesn't photograph well. "Don't look now, but here comes trouble."

"Oh, shit." Buffy Cunningham was outside the shop getting out of her car. "What the hell does she want?"

"You guys are hard to find," she said coming into the shop.

"Your intel must be faulty," said Bryan. "We're here every Saturday. I would think the FBI would know that."

"Whatever," she said not looking pleased.

"To what do we owe this visit?" I asked.

"I just wanted to give you an update. You mentioned the body glitter on the victims. I did some checking. The body glitter came from a street performer in the park. You remember that I said some idiot was throwing glitter around. He was a juggler. You've probably seen him in the park."

"Yes, I've seen him," I admitted.

"I'm bringing him in for questioning."

"I see," said Bryan. "And you think he's connected to the murders?"

"Possibly, but we know both victims were in the park and got the glitter from him. Well, I should move along now," she waved and headed back to her car.

"That was odd," said Bryan. "Why would she come by to tell us that?"

"I was just wondering the same thing," I said.

Sunday morning was warm and bright and Bryan and I drove off to pick up Dustin and Norma Jean for church. It was our custom to go to church and then out to brunch. It's also my custom to never set foot in a church unless I see a rainbow flag. The Unitarian Universalist Church has a large rainbow flag at its entrance, and it has the reputation of being a safe place for everyone.

It was summer and the service was simple, which was fine with us. It was a nice day and the church doors were open allowing in a nice fresh breeze. This morning was a treat because a folk group had been engaged to provide the music and the morning collection was being split with a local soup kitchen.

We were early for our brunch reservations, but we were seated immediately. Dustin and Norma Jean ordered bloody marys and Bryan and I ordered mimosas. This was our weekly chance to get caught up without distractions. Lately Richard had been joining us, but he was busy working on his dissertation.

"How are you doing, really?" I asked Norma Jean. We all turned to her.

"Tell us about Jenks," encouraged Bryan.

"Yes, you sort of keep him a secret," added Dustin.

"Fine," she said. "I met him when he came into the store and we got to talking. His wife is gaga in a nursing home and he was lonely. We started to talk and he asked me out like a gentleman. After the third date I was hooked. He's kind, intelligent, and good looking."

"And rich," broke in Dustin.

"Yes, and that, too. Anyway I'm in love with him. And in bed…"

"We get the picture," I said quickly and unfortunately we all were forming mental pictures and had to quickly go to our happy place to erase them.

"How about you Dustin. What's going on with you and Richard?"

"He's recovered from his injuries, but Richard is worried about his part in the murders. He's been beating himself up about whether it was something he did that tipped off the Followers. And he's working on his dissertation and hasn't had a lot of time for me."

"He'll get his degree in a couple of weeks so don't' worry. Then he'll be Dr. Hall," I tried to reassure him. "And none of this is his fault. He was recruited by the FBI and he did just as he was told. If there is a problem I'm sure it didn't start with him. The real question, Dustin, is how are you doing?"

"I feel like my life is on hold. Not much new at work to keep me occupied and all this business with murders and terrorists is all just too much."

"You know we're here for you," said Bryan and Norma Jean and I nodded agreement.

"And that," he replied with a tear forming in his eye, "means the world to me."

Chapter 15

I t was three in the morning when I heard the sirens off in the distance. At the same time Bryan's cell phone went crazy. We both jumped out of bed. I grabbed a robe and stepped out on the porch to see if I could tell what was going on while Bryan spoke on the phone.

The sky was bright in the direction of the college and I had a sinking feeling that something bad had happened. My fears were confirmed when Bryan came running out the door hastily dressed in his uniform.

"There's been an explosion at one of the office buildings on campus," he said running for his car.

"Which one?" I yelled as he took off, but he hadn't heard me. There was nothing else for me to do but get dressed and head over to the college. I had a fear in the pit of my stomach that it was the Brighton Building where the anthropology offices were.

I put the coffee pot on and jumped in the shower to try to wake up. I'm not good for much at three in the morning. I got dressed, grabbed a thermos and filled it with coffee. I took along some extra cups and jumped into my Mini Cooper and headed off toward the campus.

The police had blocked off the area around campus, so I parked on the street and walked. The police stopped me and I had to pull out my faculty ID to get by them. As I got closer I could see the building going up in flames and the firefighters trying to contain the blaze. Bryan and three of his security guards were looking on helplessly.

I took the thermos out of my backpack and poured out cups of coffee and passed them around to the men.

There were not enough cups so I drank directly out of the thermos. Once the hot coffee hit my stomach I was able to speak.

"It's the Brighton Building isn't it?" I asked.

"Yes," answered Bryan. "There was a big explosion at the north end of the building and it must have broken a gas line."

"There are priceless artifacts in my office," I said. "Not to mention the storage area of the anthropology department. At least there shouldn't be anyone in the building this time of night."

"Let's hope you're right," said Bryan.

"What happened?" I asked.

"Danny here was on duty," said Bryan indicating the tall security officer standing next to him.

"I was making my rounds of the campus," said Danny, "when I heard this loud explosion. I went to investigate and saw that the north wall had a hole blown out of it. A second explosion followed and it was followed by a fire ball. I called 911."

"Why hasn't the sprinkler system put out the fire?" I asked looking at the flames.

"That's a good question," replied Bryan.

We watched as the firefighters got the flames under control. By that time a huge crowd had gathered beyond the police barricade. Television stations had set up news cameras and the whole atmosphere was beginning to seem circus like. Smoke was billowing out of the building as the flames died down, and I was somewhat encouraged to see that the flames hadn't had time to reach the south end of the building where I had my office. Smoke damage would be bad enough.

Bryan had gone off to confer with the police and the fire departments and came back with Buffy Cunningham in tow.

"This is an FBI investigation now," she said. "The Followers have taken responsibility for the explosion. This was no accident."

It wasn't until two days later when I was allowed to get into my office. I drafted some of my students to help with the packing and moving. Extra credit was a good incentive and I had quite a crew. Artifact storage was the most important area, and I put Richard Hall in charge of the department's common storage area. Madison and I worked on clearing out my office. The offices would be moved to dorm rooms for the time being. Renovation would take all summer and if we were lucky we would be back in the Brighton Building by September. My five faculty members were clearing out their offices and carting off their computers, and I hoped they had backups of their grades because the end of the summer session was upon us.

"Looks like a lot of work," said Bryan as he entered my office and looked at the mess. "Have you lost anything?"

"Smoke damage seems to be the big thing, but other than the smell, most of my stuff survived."

"You're lucky. The social science wing is a total loss. The history and political science offices are completely destroyed."

"How terrible. What about archaeology?" I asked. Bert Higgins was off on Cape Cod.

"Safe. Their offices in the basement escaped damage."

"No water damage from the sprinkler system?"

"The system was turned off. Whoever set up the explosion wanted to make sure it wouldn't be put out."

"Whoever? I thought Buffy said the Followers took credit."

"Just because they took credit doesn't mean they did it. And all we have is one letter supposedly from the Followers, but the only source we have for that is Buffy Cunningham. Not my favorite person," added Bryan.

"Not anyone's favorite person," I agreed. "Now, if you'd like to help there's a pile of boxes over in the corner that need to be loaded onto the moving van."

A week later I was having lunch at The Roma Restaurant with Richard and Madison. They had both been extremely helpful in moving the department to the newly available dorm rooms.

"Doctors Hall and Smith," I said as they had both been awarded their degrees, "I want to thank you both for all the help you've given the department."

"You're welcome Dr. Littlefield," said Richard and Madison agreed.

"As you know this explosion has set us back a great deal and our enrollment is up." I pulled out an envelope and passed it to Madison. "This is your contract to teach cultural anthropology next semester. Unfortunately you'll have a full load of four classes."

"Thank you," she said with shining eyes as she grabbed the envelope out of my hands. It reminded me of my first teaching job.

"Richard, I just got the go ahead to add one more instructor to the department. A generous donor has given a grant for a criminal forensic researcher. You would have to teach two classes in addition to research, but I'd love to have you on my team."

"I feel like I've just won the lottery," he said stunned. "Thank you. I just wish I wasn't still a suspect."

"You're a person of interest," I reminded him. "Not a suspect. Don't be too happy you two," I warned. "I'm a real bastard to work for."

That was too much for them and they both started laughing. "Sure you are," said Richard.

"I didn't notice this before," said Madison as she held up a rib bone. We had finished setting up the temporary office and were engaged in unpacking the artifacts that Bert Higgins had sent from Cape Cod. The dorm room was small and the bed was piled with boxes of books as was most of the free space on the floor.

"What is it?" I asked as I took the magnifying glass from her hand and looked at the rib.

"It's a nick," she said. "And it looks pretty substantial.

"No wonder. It was hidden under centuries of dirt. If I'm right this goes right near the heart. You could well have discovered the cause of death."

"You think he was stabbed?"

"There is no remodeling of the damage, so he either died of the wound or shortly after."

"Murder?"

"Most likely," I said. "If it was murder, then it's lost in the mists of time."

"Is there any way we can figure out who this was?"

"Not really, but we could come close. We know the location and we can check for any historical records from the late seventeenth century and early eighteen century." That gave me an idea. "Richard would be the perfect one to do the research."

"Yes, he would. I like Richard a lot. He's professional and thorough."

"He is that," I agreed. "We need to get ready for the field work, and I'd like to get this place organized before we head to the cape."

"What do you need me to do?"

"I think we just need to label what's in each box so that when we get back into the Brighton office we can find things again."

"I'll get on it right away."

"You are Dr. Smith now," I said. "We'll get a work-study student to do this, you can supervise. Is Brad coming to the cape with you?"

"Yes, but he'll be going up to Maine to finalize the sale of the business and then joining us."

"Better hang on to him in Provincetown." I joked. "He's very good looking you know."

"Yes, I know," she replied with a grin.

Chapter 16

The FBI had rounded up the members of the Followers and charged them with acts of terrorism, but as it turned out all the members were attending a meeting when the explosion took place. Campus security cameras could not isolate any of the events leading up to the explosion, so in frustration the members were released because of lack of evidence.

"There's something just a bit off in this case," said Bryan as we boarded the flight to Boston.

"What do you mean?" I asked once we were seated and belted in.

"Two murders and an attack on a college by a group of religious fanatics? It doesn't add up. No suspects for the murders and the group that claimed responsibility for the explosion on campus was nowhere near the campus when it happened."

"They could easily have set up the explosion earlier," I said.

"Yes, but we have security cameras all around campus and yet there was no suspicious activity."

"Couldn't they have avoided the security cameras?"

"We have about a dozen of those cameras in hidden spots that are not visible. It's not likely that anyone outside of security knows where the cameras are."

"You think someone in security is responsible?"

"For the explosion and the murders? No. But maybe revealing the camera locations."

"Could someone have hacked into the security cameras and seen the areas covered by the cameras? They could then just avoid those areas and figure out what areas the cameras don't cover."

"Yes," said Bryan excitedly, "I'll bet tha's just what happened. I should call agent Cunningham and tell her."

"Don't do that yet," I said. "I want to check out something first."

"What?"

"Just a feeling I have. If we wait a bit we may have more information. Besides," I said as we watched the flight attendant demonstrate the use of seat belts, "we are on vacation."

Bryan and I were the first of the group to arrive in Provincetown. The others were to follow on later flights. We would all be staying at the Light Keepers compound. Dustin and Richard would arrive the next day, followed by Norma Jean and the recovering Jenks. Blake Carter the photographer would fly up on the weekend, as would Madison and Brad Tanner.

Bryan had never been to Provincetown, so as soon as we unpacked we took a walk down Commercial Street. Bryan's eyes were agog at the sights. Provincetown retains its outward appearance as the quintessential New England fishing village, but add to that a profusion of rainbow flags, public works of art, same sex couples walking hand in hand, gift shops, sidewalk restaurants, wide-eyed tourists and you know you're not in Kansas anymore.

"Amazing," he said as we were seated on a back deck of a restaurant that looked out over the harbor.

"How are your dancing feet?" I asked as a waiter took our order. The waiter spent a little too much time admiring Bryan, I thought.

"I haven't danced in years, why?"

"Because after we eat I'm taking you over to the Boatslip for tea dance."

"Aren't you supposed to be here working?"

"I'll check in tomorrow with Bert Higgins. But today is play day."

It was perfect New England summer weather. It was hot in the sun, comfortable in the shade and a slight breeze that held the fresh smell of the ocean. Our lunch came and we watched the activity on the fishing pier.

"This is perfect," said Bryan with a sigh.

"And all so temporary. By November the air will be icy, the tourists gone and the shops shuttered up. That's why prices are so high. The locals have only a few months to make money."

"I'll bet it's nice to be here in the winter though," considered Bryan.

"Yes, quiet and less frantic and a few places still open."

"Anything else I can do for you gentlemen?" asked the waiter as he brought the bill. "Anything at all?" and I didn't think he was talking about just the menu.

"We'll be back," I said as I handed him the payment and a rather generous tip.

Tea dance was in full swing when we got to the Boatslip. We could hear the music from the streets and after we paid the cover charge we were admitted to the party. Once again Bryan's eyes were popping out of his head. There must have been one hundred shirtless men dancing and just as many lined up against the deck railings watching the crowd.

"This is amazing," said Bryan. "I'm glad I have my sunglasses on, otherwise I might go blind."

"Let's start with a beer," I suggested. "Get an eyeful and then dance."

We made our way over to the bar where I got us two beers. Over in the corner I saw a familiar face and waved. He waved back and came over to where we were standing.

"Luke, you're back," said James.

"Bryan, this is James Cameron, the writer and poet," I said as they shook hands.

"Luke's told me about you. It's good to meet you, and he didn't exaggerate about how good looking you are," said James

"He talks too much," replied Bryan slightly embarrassed.

"If you two don't have plans tonight why don't you join me for dinner," suggested James.

I looked at Bryan who nodded, "We'd love to," I said.

"Are you at the Light Keepers?"

"Yes," replied Bryan.

"Then I'll meet you about eight."

"Sounds good," I replied.

Bryan and I joined the shirtless dancers on the dance floor until it was time to go back and get ready for dinner.

***

James came for us at eight and walked us to his house.

"I wasn't sure you could find it on your own," he said as we walked along. "The streets in this part of town follow the old cow paths and there's no parking."

"It's a nice walk," I said. "Some of these houses are very old."

"Provincetown was settled in the 1600s, but of course you know that," said James.

"Hopefully I'll know more once I start working with the archeological dig."

"This is my house here," James pointed to a small three-quarter cape house. There was a small garden in the front, and it was situated on a narrow lot with two similar houses flanking each side. Like its neighbors it was painted white with green shutters.

"Very tidy," remarked Bryan. "Looks exactly like I thought a real colonial cape would look."

James led us up the front walk which was paved with crushed oyster shells. We entered a small hallway with a winding stairway to the second floor and he took us through to the kitchen in the back of the house. There was a huge fireplace at one end of the kitchen which used to be used for cooking, and we were seated at a small scrubbed pine table. On the other side of the kitchen was a row of modern appliances among the colonial style cabinets.

"White or red?" asked James as he held up two wine bottles he had taken out of the wine cooler.

"White for me," I said

"Same for me," added Bryan. James poured three glasses of wine and sat down with us.

"I just finished your book *Crime Wave*," James said to me. "It was a fun book."

"I think it was one of his best," agreed Bryan. "A group of three incompetent thieves who bumbled every job and still managed not to get caught for three years."

"And the police who were trying to catch them were just as incompetent," I joked. "They were like Keystone Cops."

"You must have some good stories from your time in the FBI," I said to James.

"You were an FBI agent?" asked Bryan.

"Yes," James looked at me.

"I forgot to mention that," I said. "I told him about your writing and showed him some of your poetry."

"I loved some of the homoerotic images in your poems," said Bryan.

"Not everyone gets the subtlety of my poems. But I have another reason for inviting you here," said James as he took a folder off his kitchen counter and handed it to us. "I still have some friends in the agency and when Luke told me you two were working with the FBI I had one of my friends do a little digging. Why don't you look this over while I get dinner together."

Bryan grabbed the three page written report and then passed it to me when he was done.

"This is disturbing on several levels," I said when I had finished reading the report.

"Be careful," warned James. "How long are you here for?"

"About a month or so," I replied.

"Good. It wouldn't hurt to stay away from Cranmore for a while," said James as he took a pot out of the refrigerator and placed it on the stove.

Chapter 17

It was going to be a warm day, I could tell, even though the breeze from the ocean was cool. I was wearing a big floppy hat and glasses in keeping with my professor image. Bert Higgins and his interns had progressed quite a bit since my last visit.

"We've uncovered some interesting finds," said Bert as I joined him at his makeshift desk under one of the canopies set up at the dig.

"It looks like it," I observed as I looked around. There were sample holes in the ground in several places and screens made for sifting through soil set up by the tent.

"We think there are at least seven cellar holes here which leads me to believe we are dealing with a small village."

"Any water supply?" The cape had few fresh water sources.

"We think there was one well and a couple of rain water cisterns. We also uncovered a shell heap, evidence suggests an early fishing village."

"An ancient shell heap could indicate a Native American site," I said.

"Of course, but in this case we've found pottery shards and pipes which leads us to believe that it belonged to a white settlement. Take a look at this and tell me what you think."

Bert led me over to one of the excavations. It was a square hole about ten feet by ten feet and around three feet deep. I climbed down into the hole and examined the walls of the excavation. The several layers of earth and sediment were easy to see. One of the lower layers contained what looked like wood ash."

"Fire?" I asked.

"Yes, and we've found it in those cellar holes that we've dug. The layer appears to be at the same level in all the holes."

"That would mean that there was a fire that swept through the village." It was a guess but I was sure I was right.

"Correct. And there's no evidence that it was rebuilt. The next evidence we have of habitation seems to be a farm of the mid-nineteenth century."

"Did you find a graveyard?" I asked.

"No, only the one set of bones we sent you, so far at least."

"Any new artifacts?"

"Plenty. Enough to keep you out of trouble for a while." He pointed over to a large tent set up about fifty feet away.

"Great," I said and looked at my watch. "I have to go to the airport and pick up some members of my party and then I'll get started."

The Provincetown airport is a small landing strip out in the dunes of Provinceland by the beach. Richard and Dustin had elected to take the small prop plane from Boston rather than drive down. They had Blake Carter with them as well.

Norma Jean and Jenks would fly in tomorrow and Brad and Madison would arrive by car sometime today.

"You guys look tired," I said as they got off the plane.

"We took the red eye from LA to Boston. Then this egg beater from Boston," said Dustin.

"Let's get you settled in," said Bryan as he and I loaded their luggage into the rental car.

"We're staying at the Light Keepers," I said as Bryan slipped behind the wheel. "It's a compound of three large inns and you'll be with us in the men's only building."

"It's clothing optional," added Bryan with a wink.

"Naked men?" asked Dustin with a little more interest.

"Yes," I answered, "but not all men should be seen naked."

"That's for sure," said Blake.

"Anyway, after you're settled we'll take you to lunch and give you a tour of downtown," I said. "Actually Bryan, drive down to the other end of town and drive up Commercial Street."

"Sure thing."

Commercial Street is one way because it is too narrow to allow more than one car at a time. And the ride is slow because of the foot traffic and the occasional lack of sidewalks. I pulled down the vanity mirror on the sun shade so I could watch the reactions of the three of them in the back seat.

"Amazing," said Richard who I was pretty sure hadn't seen anything like this.

"Sort of like San Francisco," said Dustin.

"I can't wait to get out there with my camera," added Blake.

After our sightseeing trip through downtown we grabbed some sandwiches at a small sandwich shop and brought them back to the inn and had lunch outside in the shade. Then I left them to themselves and headed over to the dig.

"Well, look who showed up," Bert Higgins greeted me.

"Any new discoveries since this morning?"

"A few. We put them in the tent with the other artifacts. We've catalogued some of our finds but we need you to make some sense of them."

"Let me get started. Madison Smith and Richard Hall will be with me tomorrow, and we should be able to make some progress."

"A little bird told me that you've hired them for your department."

"Your little bird is correct," I replied. "How did you find out so fast?"

"Social media of course."

"Of course." I headed into the tent and eyeballed the artifacts that had been brought in. Most were still encrusted with dirt and not recognizable at present. I would carefully have to clean each one and then try to figure out what it was used for or what part in played in daily life.

I picked up a small cylindrical piece of iron that was tapered at one end. It was a rare find, a goffering iron. These irons were used to iron the ornate neck ruffs of gentlemen's collars. What made the find unusual was the fact that it was an older style of dress, more at home in the early 1600s than the later 1600s.

By the time I had the iron cleaned and catalogued, Bert brought in several more items. "Lots of pieces of pottery," he said as he placed them on the large artifact table.

"Those are actually pieces of china," I said just to annoy him. "Pottery is much more primitive."

"No shit, I was just using a generic term."

"Of course," I agreed with a hint of irony.

"Well, I'll let you get back to work," he said as he swished away.

I moved on and picked up a rusted mess of iron. It was hard to distinguish but it appeared to be a pile of handmade iron nails. Nails were expensive and used mostly by the wealthier colonist. Most joining was done with wooden pegs because of the expense, thus finding a pile of unused nails was somewhat of a mystery. There appeared to be wood ash mixed in with the dirt and rust which led me to think that maybe this was a box of nails that had been in a fire, since there was evidence of a large fire at the site. I left the pile for Madison and Richard to clean and separate. I looked at my watch and it was time to go.

By the time I got to the inn Madison and Brad had arrived. They were staying at one of the other of the inn's buildings away from the men's building. Brad had made dinner reservations for all of us, so we headed out to a restaurant near the east end. It was a long walk, but the reviews were good, and when we arrived we were taken to a table with a nice harbor view.

Once we were seated and ordered our first round of drinks we all relaxed. I gave a report about what was happening at the dig, which was why we were in Provincetown to begin with. Of course it really was a working vacation for Madison, Richard and me. The rest were here to enjoy time away.

"Well, I have some news from West Hollywood," said Richard. "According to agent Cunningham, the FBI are closing in on the Followers and expect an arrest soon."

Bryan and I looked at each other. "That's interesting," Bryan said. "Did she name a suspect?"

"Barbara Levesque," he answered. "She and her husband were at the motel when Amanda Springer was killed, and no one saw her at the motel when her husband was murdered."

"I saw her at the motel," I said.

"Yes, but you went back to your room around the time he was killed, so you couldn't say for sure that she was working the desk for the entire time."

"Something doesn't seem right," said Bryan.

"It seems to be too easy," I added.

"Sometimes," said Richard, "the easy answer is the right one."

We ordered dinner and Blake told us of his plans to photograph Provincetown, and Dustin told us about a new client of his who was a movie producer.

"And Ian Stoddard will be coming to Hollywood to make a new film in the fall," said Dustin with a wicked smile. Ian was an old boyfriend and an out Scottish actor.

"Interesting," was all I could say. "What type of movie?"

"An action movie. Something about a child kidnapping."

"I think that's been done," said Bryan with an edge to his voice. He wasn't a big fan of Ian's knowing my history with him.

"If you remember," I said to remind Bryan, "I had a choice to make and I chose you."

"So you did," he said smiling, "So you did."

"Brad, when are you heading back up to Maine?" asked Blake.

"After the weekend. I need to settle up the Maine business and then I'll be back,"

"Are you really selling the funeral home?" asked Dustin.

"I think so. My life is on the west coast now."

Our dinners arrived and the conversation turned to how we would spend our leisure time on Cape Cod.

Chapter 18

It was a cool morning with a breeze off the water, but the sun was bright and hot and it promised to be a hot summer day. Since moving to California I've learned that heat is a relative term. A hot day in New England is whenever the temperature reaches eighty, unlike a hot day in Las Vegas at plus one hundred. The problem with New England is the humidity. Whenever the dew point shoots above sixty the atmosphere becomes uncomfortable. Still I was grateful for the smell of the Atlantic regardless of the weather.

"Got something for you," said Bert Higgins, whose crew was already at work when I arrived.

"You're here early," I said as I took the object out of his hands and placed it on the table. It was rusty and dirty, but I could easily see what it was by the shape.

"I thought we would start early and knock off for the day if it gets hot. Channel seven was predicting a steamy day."

"Where did you find this?" I asked.

"It was in the ground where we dug up the bones."

"This could be the murder weapon."

"Murder? Who was murdered?"

"You didn't read my report, did you? We found a nick in one of the ribs. It was near the heart. The man died of a knife wound, and I'll bet we can match the knife to the wound."

"This should make for an interesting story," Bert was fairly beaming. "Imagine the publicity I'm going to get out of this."

"You might want to hold off on this for a while," I replied. "We need to know more before we jump the gun."

"You're right. There might be even more information we can dig up."

Just then my cell phone went off. I looked at the caller ID. "I need to take this," I said and stepped outside the tent.

"Agent Cunningham, what can I do for you?"

"I thought I'd let you know that we've arrested Barbara Lévesque for the murders. No need for you to bother with this anymore."

"Yes, Richard told me," I said.

"Richard is there? That's good."

"Well, I should go. I've got work to do," I said and got her off the phone. Why was she calling me?

"Good morning," said Madison and she handed me a cup of coffee.

"Thanks, good morning. We've got a new development." I told her about the knife. "If you would clean it up we'll try to match it with the nick in the ribs. I have a close up of the rib on my laptop. If we take a photo of the knife we can superimpose the images on the screen."

"This is awesome," she said with enthusiasm. "Imagine a centuries old mystery."

"History is mystery."

"Poet and don't know it," she said and entered the tent and got to work.

By late afternoon we had cleaned the knife blade and about a dozen pieces of pottery. Bert Higgins came in with a few arrow heads he had uncovered. My eyes glaze over when I see arrowheads. I spent one summer in college on a dig in Maine as part of my archeology requirement. Sifting through metric yards of dirt to find an arrowhead or two was about as fun as raking blueberries in the hot sun.

"This is an interesting find," he said as he set the arrowheads on the table.

"Native Americans lived on Cape Cod for thousands of years," I said.

"Yes, and these," he said pointing to three smaller arrowheads, "are common in this region. But these," here he indicated four larger arrowheads, "are from the southern region. These are not typical finds here at all."

"More mysteries," said Madison with excitement.

"So it would appear," I said.

"Good luck with your narrative," said Bert with a wave as he left.

"Interesting character," said Madison.

"Did you ever have a class with him?" I asked.

"Just an undergraduate introductory course. It was okay."

"He's single," I said teasingly.

"I don't doubt that at all," she laughed.

"How was your day?" I woke up from my nap and found a very naked Bryan Sullivan sprawled out on the bed next to me.

"Tiring. I'm not used to working outside in the fresh air. We've got lots of puzzle pieces and no clear idea about how it all fits."

"Isn't that the fun part?"

"It's fun, yes, but also a test of my skills."

"You have a murder that's about three hundred and fifty years old." Bryan slipped on a pair of shorts and headed to the coffee maker in the room. I watched him walk across the room. That man is gorgeous. "I'll need some coffee to hear this story," he said.

"Bert Higgins uncovered some bones in a shallow grave when his group first started the dig. He sent them to me to identify, thinking, I'm sure, that they were Native American remains. Examination of the skull showed that it was the skull and bones of a Caucasian male in his early thirties. The dry, sandy soil had preserved the bones to a remarkable degree. Time had, of course, leached out minerals, but the structure was still identifiable."

"I see. So this was an extraordinary find?"

"It certainly was. When we had time to examine the remains closely, having to move my office to a dorm room didn't help, Madison discovered a nick on one of the ribs near the heart. There was no remodeling of the bone there, so we determined that it was either the cause of death, or that he died shortly after the wound. Remember there were no antibiotics back then so the wound could have become infected and caused his death."

"But you don't think he died of infection."

"Bert Higgins and his crew went back to the site for further excavation and uncovered a knife blade. Using computer generated graphics we could show that the blade and the nick in the ribs were a perfect fit."

"So murder?"

"Yes, indeed."

"Have you noticed, Luke, that you seem to attract murder?"

"Occupational hazard. I'm an anthropologist after all. Most of the people and cultures I study are dead."

"So what do you do next?"

"Nothing much. I need to classify the artifacts and recreate daily life in Colonial Cape Cod. In addition I have to show that there were other uses of the land, too. After the village disappeared there was a farm on the land, so I need to address that also. I'm sending Richard out to research as much as he can about the site."

"The upside of all your work is that I get to be here in Provincetown."

After breakfast at the inn Bryan and I drove out to the airport and picked up Jenks Carter and Norma Jean. Norma Jean stepped off the plane like a fifties movie star. She was wearing a wide skirt and a scarf over her head and large dark glasses. Jenks was wearing what appeared to be a nineteen seventies leisure suit. Fortunately this was Provincetown where eccentricities were the norm.

"That flight sucked!" said Norma Jean by way of greeting when she stepped off the plane.

"And welcome to Provincetown," Bryan returned her greeting.

"Hi, guys," said Jenks as he struggled with several carry-on pieces of luggage. Norma Jean was not a light packer.

"How was your flight?" I asked politely.

"I slept through most of it," replied Jenks.

"Alcohol helped," added Norma Jean.

Bryan and I took the luggage from Jenks and loaded the luggage and the passengers into the car. The bags were even heavier than we first thought. How an octogenarian like Jenks got them on board was a mystery. He must be in pretty good shape for an old guy.

"We'll take you to the inn so you can rest up," I said as I got behind the wheel.

"Rest up?" sputtered Norma Jean. "We're here to party. We can rest up when we're dead."

"Well this is Provincetown," said Bryan. "People sleep in. Nothing happens until noon."

"Party! Party! Party," the two of them chanted in the back seat.

"Keep it up and I'll stop the car," I threatened.

"You're harshing my buzz," grumbled Norma Jean.

"Buzzed?" I asked. "It's ten o'clock in the morning."

"It's five o'clock somewhere," added Jenks.

"If you want," Bryan slipped into tough cop mode, "we can take you back to the airport."

"Queens be bitchy," chimed in Norma Jean.

It seemed like a long way back to the inn, but we got the two of them settled into their room in the third house and Bryan and I went over to the men's section. It was a good beach day and the other guests were getting ready to head off to the beach at Herring Cove.

"You guys going off to the beach?" asked Dave the owner.

"I have to work," I said. "But Blake, Brad, Bryan, and Dustin are going, but Richard, Madison and I have lots to do."

"I wish you could go," said Bryan.

"I want a full report, and we'll plan on going with you guys tomorrow." I left the little group and joined Richard and Madison on the front porch.

"Dr. Hall and Dr. Smith, I think we have to spend today cleaning and organizing the artifacts. It's not the most glamorous part of the job, but necessary. Richard, I want you to start the research tomorrow. Start with the local historical society and then I'm sending you to Boston to check on any records you can find there."

"I'll be sort of a history detective," he said.

"Yes indeed you will."

We got in the car and drove off to the site. Bert and his interns were already hard at work. Something had been bothering me about the site and I decided to ask Bert about it.

"Good morning, Luke," Bert's greeting was more animated than usual.

"Good morning. Bert something about this site is bothering me."

"What's that?"

"If this was a fishing village, which all indications have shown, why have you found only one grave?"

"Yes, that's bothered me, too. There should be a graveyard around here, but we haven't found it."

"What's your theory?"

"Over there," he pointed to a place just beyond the trees. There were two large Victorian summer cottages just over the hill.

"You think the houses were built on the graveyard?"

"It's the most likely spot."

"Anyway to tell?"

"If the owners will let us look around, we might find it."

"And that brings up another point. Why wasn't the body we found buried in the graveyard?"

"I'm sure you have a theory," Bert looked at me over his glasses.

"I have a few ideas, but I need to study this just a little more," I said mysteriously just to be a prick.

Chapter 19

J ames Cameron had left me a text message to call him, but since cell service was hit or miss on the outer cape, I didn't get the message until I returned from the dig site. I called him back as soon as I got back to the inn and changed out of my dirty clothes.

"Hey James, what's up?" I said when I got hold of him.

"Hi Luke. I'd like to meet you and Bryan for drinks later. I've got something you might be interested in."

"Like what?" I asked.

"I can't say over the phone. Let's meet at the Post Office Cabaret on Commercial Street for drinks. You know where that is?" The post office was the name of an establishment that offered both food and alcohol. Its decor consisted of post office boxes and related items.

"What time?"

"About 5:30."

"Okay, we'll see you there."

Bryan came into the room just as I hung up. "How was your day at the beach?" I asked.

"Fun and sun."

"Let's grab a beer and go out to the backyard and you can tell me about it." I grabbed two beers out of the mini fridge and headed out to the backyard where Bryan found two lawn chairs with a view of the hot tub and several men frolicking in it.

"The beach was interesting to say the least. First we had to practically step over the topless lesbians on the first section of beach. It was a long walk but we found the men's area. The sand was nice and warm, but the water was far too cold to go swimming."

"I think it warms up for a few days in August," I said. "I know in Maine survival time in the surf in June is about five minutes."

"The three of us decided to take a walk in the dunes."

"I know what's coming."

"Yes, there was nude sunbathing in the dunes."

"And?"

"And yes, there was sex in the dunes."

"Did you guys watch?"

"Of course we did, but by that time we were getting sunburned and it was time to come back."

"James Cameron called and wants us to meet him for drinks. He said he had something to share but wouldn't say what it was."

"Intriguing."

We spotted James at a table in the back of the Post Office Cabaret. He had another man with him. I could tell the man was tall even though he was seated and his blond hair stood out like a light in the darkness. James spotted us and waved us over.

"Max, this is Luke Littlefield and Bryan Sullivan." We shook hands. "Max Bailey is an old friend of mine from my FBI days. Have a seat guys."

The waiter came over and fetched Bryan and me a beer. James and Max already had theirs.

"I was interested in getting your take on the murders in West Hollywood," Max said.

"I don't understand," I said confused. "I thought Barbara Levesque was arrested for the murders."

"Acts of terrorism is of concern, but the agency in California doesn't seem to be getting anywhere, and we have our concerns about agent Cunningham. We've had to let Barbara Levesque go for lack of solid evidence. The agent in charge seems to be a little too eager for an arrest and didn't have enough evidence to show guilt."

"You better explain," said Bryan taking on a business tone.

"All we have really to go on is a statement made to the press by the Followers that they were responsible for the explosion at Cranmore. When we rounded them up they denied it, and all the known members had solid alibis."

"That doesn't mean they didn't do it," I added.

"Of course not," Max replied. "But the statement to the press seems to be missing."

"Missing?" Bryan looked at Max quizzically.

"It was a typed letter sent to the *LA Times*. The police took the letter and somehow in the transfer to the FBI the letter went missing."

"Who's taking the blame?" I asked.

"Neither the police of the FBI."

Bryan just shook his head. "How can we help?"

"I was hoping you'd ask," said Max and then he told us the plan.

We all decided to have dinner together since this was the first time we were all together in Provincetown. Blake would be staying here for two weeks taking photos,

Brad would be heading up to Maine tomorrow, Richard and Madison were here for the summer to help with the dig, I would be flying back to California every few weeks to get the anthropology department ready for the fall semester, and Bryan had to go back to his security position in a week. Jenks and Norma Jean had no plans, they said, and would stay as long as they liked.

We met on the porch of the inn and had some wine before we headed out for dinner. We chose Napi's Restaurant downtown because of the good food and the quirky décor, Mercifully Provincetown has no chain restaurants and every restaurant and cafe is unique. Once we were seated we ordered more wine and checked out the menu.

"What's everyone doing tomorrow?" asked Brad. "What will I be missing?"

"We're going on a tour of the dunes," said Norma Jean. "They have these huge SUVs and they take us out on an historic dunes tour."

"And I get to snuggle with my sweetie," said Jenks throwing Norma Jean a wink. I think she actually blushed.

"I'm going to take my camera and climb Pilgrims' Monument," said Blake.

"Us, too," said Dustin and nodded to Richard.

"You realize that it's two hundred and fifty feet high and has one hundred and sixty-six steps?" I asked.

"How do you know that?" asked Bryan looking at be dubiously.

"I just read it last night in a guide book," I admitted.

"We should go, too," said Bryan.

"As long as we go in the afternoon. I have to get over to the dig in the morning."

"Do they have an elevator?" asked Norma Jean.

"No they don't," said Richard.

"We're out," said Jenks and Norma Jean nodded.

"We'll find something else to do," added Norma Jean as her hand disappeared under the table near Jenks.

We ordered dinner and a second glass of wine. No one was driving.

"So give us an update on the dig," asked Blake. "And I want to come out later this week and take some photos."

"Having a famous photographer for the dig would be awesome," I replied.

"Actually I've arranged to have a photo spread of the find in *History Today*. I think that would be good for Cranmore."

"Oh yes," I said. "It would indeed. And here's a good angle for the story: murder in Colonial Provincetown.

"Murder?" asked everyone in unison.

"We have remains with evidence that the victim was stabbed, and we have the murder weapon," I explained.

"So what's the story?" asked Blake.

"We have to do more research, especially of historic records, but so far we can surmise that there was a small village on the site. We have a shell heap with colonial artifacts that tells us this was probably a fishing village. The artifacts are consistent with the mid to late seventeenth century. There is a layer of ash and charcoal in the earth's strata which indicates a fire. The archeologists have identified about a dozen foundations, all with ash residue in a layer of earth."

"So the village burned?" asked Jenks.

"That is the most plausible explanation."

"What about the murder?" asked Norma Jean. "I love a good murder."

"The first thing that I received was the skull. It was the skull of a Caucasian male about the age of thirty. The interesting thing about it was the age of the skull. It was well preserved because of the dry sandy soil of the cape."

"You can tell all that by the skull?" asked Blake.

"Sex, age, and race were easy," I explained. "The age of the skull, however, was harder to pinpoint. That took further testing at a lab."

"What about the murder?" asked Dustin.

"We were sent more bones later and Madison noticed a nick in one of the ribs near the heart. There was no remodeling of the bone, so we knew that the wound was either fatal or occurred shortly before death. Bert Higgins and his interns did some further digging and uncovered a rusty blade. We tested the blade against the nick in the ribs and it was a perfect fit."

"This will make a great story," exclaimed Blake. "Can I get some photos of the rib and blade?"

"Yes, of course. But the mystery doesn't end there," I added. Richard and Madison nodded.

"How so?" asked Brad.

"The body was in a shallow grave, not near any other graves, and we've been unable to find the village graveyard. And why would a murder victim be buried with the knife that probably killed him?"

"And you think you can find out?" asked Jenks.

"I'm sending Richard to Boston for some historical research. Maybe we can uncover something," I said as our meals arrived.

Chapter 20

It was a clear and sunny afternoon. I left Madison at the dig with the artifacts and met the guys in the parking lot of the Pilgrim Monument. The monument is the tallest granite structure in the country and was built to commemorate the landing of the Pilgrims. It was here in the harbor where they signed the Mayflower Compact. The tower was began in 1907 when President Theodore Roosevelt laid the cornerstone.

We first visited the small museum of Provincetown history before beginning the climb to the top. The climb was not as bad as I thought. There were ramps and stairs and on the way we got to view various stones donated by states and cities and towns. It took us about fifteen minutes to reach the top, but the view was spectacular. We could see for miles in all direction. I was sorry I hadn't thought to bring along a pair of binoculars.

Looking at the beauty around me I was unhappy that I had to leave and fly back to California tomorrow, though I would be back in a few days. I had worked it that I only had to fly back twice during my stay in Provincetown.

I needed to attend an important faculty meeting, and I had to oversee the transfer of the department from temporary storage in the dorm back to the restored department offices. While I was there, I thought I'd touch base with Buffy Cunningham and see what was new in the Followers case.

That evening we had an informal dinner at the inn. Richard went to a local sandwich shop and picked up sandwiches for all of us. Later Bryan, Dustin, Blake,

Richard and I decided to check out late night on Commercial Street. Night time in Provincetown is true street theater. We ended up outside of Spiritus Pizza. We ordered a large cheese pizza and sat on the steps outside to eat it. Spiritus is a local gathering spot and there must have been thirty men and women hanging around of all different ages. Buford Chase was there among the crowd.

"Where's the rest of the poets" I asked.

"Over that the A House, I think."

"This is Blake Carter," I said introducing the two.

"Buford Chase," he said as they shook hands.

"Blake is a famous photographers to the stars," added Bryan.

"And Buford," I said, "is a nationally known reporter."

"Have some pizza," said Dustin as he passed the pizza box over to Buford.

"Thanks," he said as he took a piece. "Best pizza this side of New York."

"It is delicious," I admitted. "A great late night snack."

"And they're open very late," said Richard as he glanced at the hours listed by the door.

"Well," said Blake as we finished the last piece of pizza, "I think I'll scout around and see if I can find some night time places to photograph."

"Need some company?" asked Buford.

"That would be great," said Blake who suddenly became shy. "You probably know the town inside out."

"I know a few places that are nice late at night," Buford replied. I didn't see either of them again that night.

***

"Sons of bitches," spewed Norma Jean when she came into to the breakfast room for coffee in the morning. "Damn honeymooners in the next room banging the headboard all night."

"All night?" I asked skeptically as I went to the buffet and refilled my coffee cup.

"Well at least until ten o'clock."

"Ten o'clock is not all night," I reminded her.

"Well, I go to bed early. I need my beauty sleep. You don't get this," she said pointed to herself, "without work."

"You need to work harder," I said under my breath.

"What's that?"

"I said you need more coffee. Where's Jenks?"

"He's sleeping in. We used one of his blue pills last night and he needs his rest. I'm one hot number, you know."

"You are a handful," I admitted.

"There you are," said Bryan as he walked into the breakfast room. "Are you ready for the airport?"

"I guess," I said. "My bags are there in the corner."

"Let's go."

"Can I trust you with all these pretty boys here in Provincetown?" I asked as we got into the car.

"I get to sleep with an underwear model with a PhD. Why would I want any of this local riff raft?"

"Good answer. So what are you doing today?"

"The guys and I are going on a whale watch. I wish you were going."

"It's only for a few days, and when I get back I want to go to the beach."

The flight to Boston was very short and the flight to LAX was very long. I was tired when I got home. The house had that smell that closed up houses have. I opened the windows to air out the place, fired up the Mini cooper and headed over to Kelsey's Pub for beer and a burger. Even though it was only nine o'clock in California, my body was on east coast time and I wanted to go to bed.

I woke up early the next day still not adjusted to the time change, and I realized all my friends were a whole continent away and I was on my own. I had nothing to eat in the house, so I made myself a cup of coffee and headed out to the coffee shop for breakfast.

Everything was quiet when I arrived on campus even though summer session was in full swing. I had a visitor waiting for me in my newly refurbished office as I opened the door.

"Ian?" I said in surprise. "What are you doing here?" I knew Ian Stoddard was due to film a movie in Hollywood, but I didn't know when that would be.

"Good morning, Luke," he said as he gave me a hug. "I wanted to surprise you."

"You certainly did that, Ian. It's good to see you."

"You're looking even more handsome than ever, if that's possible. What the hell happened here?" he asked as he looked around at the boxes piled everywhere.

"We had an explosion and a fire. They had to move my stuff to a dorm while the office was being fixed up. I just arrived yesterday to try and get the department back in order before the fall term."

"Back from where?"

"I've been at an archeological dig on Cape Cod."

"Well, I've come to invite you and Bryan out for dinner."

"Bryan is still out on the cape. I'll be going back in a few days."

"Even better. I'll have you all to myself."

"I don't want to end up in the tabloids again. The last time I had dinner with you the press inferred that I was your rent boy."

"I'm not of interest to the press right now. They have other celebrities to deal with. Rumor has it that a former Olympic medal winner has a surprise."

"I don't think it will be much of a surprise," I replied.

"Probably not," he laughed. "I'll pick you up at eight."

"Fine," I agreed. "Now I have work to do." He gave me another hug before he left. Not only was the man good looking, but he had an aura of confidence that I hadn't noticed before.

I gathered up a team of work-study students and set them to unpacking the boxes and set up the offices. Workmen were still working on the restoration and the sounds of hammers and drills filled the air. I had them take a large office and divide it into two smaller offices for Richard and Madison. The anthropology department would now have five full time instructors and several adjunct faculty members. My department was one of the largest on campus, something that I was proud of.

By five o'clock we had made significant progress; so much so that I believed we would only need one more day to finish the move and allow me to go back to the cape a day early.

I went home, called Bryan, vacuumed the house, showered and was dressed by the time Ian came to take me to dinner. He was dressed in formal attire, and I made him wait while I changed into something more formal than the jeans I had put on.

"Where are you taking me?" I asked.

"It's a surprise. You look great by the way."

"You, too. But then you are a movie star."

"One who is being escorted by the best looking male model on the west coast."

"Flattery," I said, "is greatly appreciated."

We got into his car, a red BMW, and headed off into the Hollywood Hills. After about forty minutes we pulled into what looked like an exclusive country club. I could tell because the valets wore uniforms and all the cars were high end imports. We were greeted by a tuxedoed maître d' and shown to a table that had more crystal and silver than a Rodeo Drive jewelry store. A waiter appeared with two martinis and a menu. The menu had no prices listed.

"This is a little out of my league," I said once I put my menu down and looked around.

"Nonsense, you look like a million bucks."

"I suppose there are famous people here dining?"

"Quite a few. Look around."

I looked but didn't see anyone familiar. "You know I don't watch TV or movies."

"Yes," he sighed. "You didn't know who I was when you met me either."

"That's true," I admitted. "Now tell me why I'm here."

"This is the place to be seen. I'm filming a new movie next week, and I want to make sure people know I'm back. And what better excuse than that to have your company for a few hours."

"I did tell Bryan I was having dinner with you, by the way."

"I want to hate Bryan, but I can't. He's a good guy."

"He is that."

"So what are you up to? You haven't stumbled on any more bodies have you?" He was referring to my unfortunate habit of discovering murders..

"Well actually there have been a few incidences."

"A few incidences?"

I told him about the murders related to the Followers and about the recently discovered bones on the cape.

"So let me get this straight. You and your friends are involved with an FBI investigation of two murders, an arson case, and a four hundred year old mysterious death?"

"It sounds much worse when you say it." Ian had a melodic voice with a Scottish accent. The waiter appeared and we both ordered prime rib and lobster.

"So you better explain," replied Ian.

"Well, it started when I had an undercover FBI agent in my class?"

"Why was he in your class?"

"He's a she. Supposedly she was there to check out the college's compliance with federal laws regarding the reporting of crimes."

"And she needed to be undercover for that?" Ian was looking at me with those wide amazing blue eyes that had helped make him a star.

"Well it turns out that was just a cover story. She was really there to investigate a religious cult called the Followers. The FBI had information that they were planning something big."

"And how did that involve you?"

"It didn't. At least not at first. It was Dustin that got us involved."

"Dustin?"

"His boyfriend Richard went missing. Richard is one of my grad students and a former military intelligence officer. He had been recruited by the FBI to infiltrate the Followers on campus because of his intelligence background."

"So Richard went missing?"

"Sort of," I explained. "He was helping a young woman get away from the Followers, and he hid her in a motel. He went out to buy groceries and when he returned the young woman was gone and there was the corps of another young women in his room."

"I'm not sure I follow."

"The FBI believe it was an attempt to frame Richard. Somehow the Followers figured out that he might be an infiltrator. The young woman he tried to help out was one of the leaders of the followers. It turns out the motel was run by two other leaders of the Followers."

I was interrupted in my narrative by the appearance of our dinner salads. It was one of my favorites, a wedge of iceberg lettuce with bacon bits and blue cheese.

"Did they arrest Richard?"

"They did at first to make it appear to the group that they were successful in their framing of him. But they knew he didn't do it. Richard was able to identify the young woman who set him up and it turned out that she had a long police record." I looked down and my salad was gone and I didn't remember eating it. I needed to slow down, so I took a deep breath.

"So that was the first murder?" asked Ian as he finished the last of his salad.

"Yes, and they thought they could arrest the two motel owners for the crime, but they had alibis for the time of the murder." The uniformed waiter whisked away our salad plates and replaced them with cups of broth.

"I'm still not clear how you got involved."

"Bryan, as you know, left the police force to open an antique shop. He missed the work so he took the position of head of campus security when it became available. Because the murder involved a Cranmore graduate student, he got involved. And of course Dustin is my best friend and Richard is his boyfriend.

"Buffy Cunningham, the FBI agent, wanted to use me to distract the wife of the motel couple while she distracted the husband. It was an attempt to make them both jealous and hopefully get some information."

"This Buffy person used you as bait?"

"Basically."

"So what happened?"

"She was to meet the husband, but he was discovered murdered."

"You do have an interesting life," he said as our steak and lobster dinner arrived.

After dinner Ian drove us out to the beach. It was late at night and we were still dressed in formal attire. We both took off our shoes and walked along the beach dressed as we were.

"What about the murder on Cape Cod?" he asked.

"We're collecting historical evidence of a colonial fishing village. Professor Higgins and his interns came across some bones. My assistant and I noticed a nick on one of the ribs and further excavation uncovered a blade that fit the nick in the rib. The body was also not buried in the local graveyard as near as we can tell."

"Do you think you can solve that one?" asked Ian.

"Not a chance," I said, "Unless we uncover more evidence and after almost four hundred years that would take a lot of luck."

"It's getting late," said Ian as I turned to face him in the moonlight. "I don't suppose you'd like to come back to my place?"

"As much as I'd like to," I admitted, "I have this great guy in my life and I wouldn't mess that up for the world."

Ian grabbed me and kissed me. "I understand. Let's go and I'll drop you off. Can we still be friends?"

"Count on it," I said as I took his hand.

Chapter 21

Trying to get my office back in order was proving more time-consuming than I had originally thought. I was unpacking the documents I needed to start the fall semester and was trying to make sure I had them all. The work-study students had been helpful in moving and unpacking, but it was up to me to put my desk back in order and make sure I had all the files I needed.

In the last box, at the bottom, I found a copy of the Levesque autopsy. I picked it up and read it again. Something about it was still bothering me. Levesque had cuts on the bottom of his feet and pieces of broken glass embedded in his flesh. Why was he barefoot? Why did he run? I decided to call the medical examiner's office and speak to Mary Brooks.

"Dr. Littlefield," she said when she answered her extension, "What can I do for you?"

"Hello, Dr. Brooks. I was just reading through the autopsy report on Joshua Levesque. I'm trying to make sense of the broken glass and the cuts on his feet. I see that death was caused by a bullet to the chest."

"Yes, the blow to the head was first, but not enough to kill him, just stun him."

"I don't know where the glass comes in."

"Well, the glass was auto glass."

"Automobile glass?"

"Yes. Auto glass is tempered. It doesn't break into sharp pieces like regular glass. When it breaks it breaks into pebble sized pieces that causes much less damage."

"So it was a windshield?"

"No, it wasn't. A windshield, in addition to being tempered, is laminated. There is a layer of plastic film between glass layers. The film keeps the glass from flying around and causing more damage. No, the glass was from a rear car window."

I thought for a moment. "Do you think he kicked out a rear window?"

"That is the most likely scenario."

"If he kicked out the window and then crawled out, why wasn't the rest of him cut up?"

"His feet took the brunt of the damage. The rest of the glass would have been small pebble shaped round pieces. We did find some fine pieces of glass in his clothing."

"Thanks for the information," I said. A picture was beginning to form in my mind, and I didn't like where this was going.

"Anytime, Luke," she said and hung up.

I tried to pay attention to what was being said at the faculty meeting, but my mind was elsewhere. The dean was going over facts and figures about enrollment for the coming fall semester. I couldn't help but think about the Levesque murder. Barbara Levesque was accused of the crime, and I was confident that she didn't do it, even though she was one of the local cult leaders. If only I had kept a closer eye on her at the motel and not gone off to my room for a nap. But then again I didn't know that her husband would get himself murdered, did I?

I was sure she was at the motel, but I couldn't prove it. Then a thought struck me. Maybe someone at the motel saw her during the time her husband was murdered. But of course the police would have checked that wouldn't they? It was worth a trip over to the motel to check. Not all people who live in motels are trustful of police.

I left the college just as the faculty meeting was winding down and drove over to the Sky View Motel. I was greeted at the front desk by a young woman who bore a striking resemblance to Barbara Levesque.

"May I help you?" she asked.

"My name is Luke Littlefield. I'm an anthropology professor and I'm looking into the death of Joshua Levesque."

The young woman was about to say something. I stopped her before she could start.

"I think Barbara is innocent. I know the police had to let her go because of lack of evidence, but she's still a suspect. I'd like to help." I saw the young woman visibly relax.

"I'm her sister Grace. I'm looking after the motel. How can I help?"

"I was staying here at the time of the murder. Your sister was here at the time, but I can't prove she was here the whole time."

"You didn't see her?"

"Yes, I saw her, but I went back to my room for the two hour span when the murder supposedly took place."

"What do you need?"

"I need a list of the residents who were here the day of the murder. I know you have some full-timers staying here."

"I'm not supposed to give out that information."

"Your sister is a murder suspect," I reminded her.

She went to the desktop computer and punched in some keys. "I have to run to the store room. I'll be gone about fifteen minutes," she said and left.

I stepped behind the counter and looked at the screen. It was a list of the residents of the motel. I jotted down the names and room numbers. Stepping outside the motel office I looked around to see which rooms had a clear view of the office. There were several, so I checked the room numbers against the names. Three of the rooms had permanent guests.

Room 222 was on the second floor across from the office so I took the outside staircase to the second floor and knocked on the door.

"Hey, man," said a middle age man with long hair and love beads and whom I suspected was a stoner.

"Billy Banister?" I asked as I looked at my list.

"That's my name, don't wear it out," he laughed at his own joke.

"My name is Luke Littlefield. I wonder if I might ask you some questions."

"You a cop?"

"No, I'm a friend of the Levesque's," I said stretching the truth.

"Okay, come on in." The room was neat, but had peace posters and antidrug posters on the wall that looked like they belonged back in 1968. Ironically there where posters supporting the legalization of marijuana. I guess Mr. Bannister didn't see weed as a gateway drug. Neither did I. "Wine?" he offered.

"Sure," I said. He went to the small refrigerator and grabbed a bottle of wine. He poured the wine out into two paper cups and passed me one. I took a swallow. The wine was similar to the wine I drank in college. Cheap to be sure. I reached into my pocket and grabbed my phone and hit record. I was confident that Billy Banister was not tech savvy. I put the phone back in my pocket.

"What do you want to know?"

"I noticed you have a good view of the office. I wonder if you remember where you were when Joshua was killed?" From his chair he had a great view of the motel office and the street from the large picture window of his room.

"I was here. I don't go out much," he said. "It's crazy out there. Lots of sons-of-bitches running around."

"Did you see Barbara leave the office at all that day?" I asked to get back on track.

"No, she didn't leave. I could see into the office and she was there all day. Toke?" he asked holding up a joint.

"No thank you."

"I can see her car from here too. It never moved."

"Did you tell the police this?" I asked.

"Nope. I don't talk to the cops. When I saw them arrive I took off and stayed with my buddy Jim up in LA."

"They really need to know this," I said. "They think Barbara killed her husband."

"But they let her go," he said as he inhaled the smoke.

"They didn't have enough evidence to hold her, but she hasn't been cleared. You can clear her if you tell the police what happened."

"Well," he sighed. "I guess I could talk to them seeing as Barbara has always been nice to me."

"That would be great," I said. "It might be better if you went down to the police station instead of having them come here." I made a gesture with my hand indicating the smoke-filled room.

I got up to go when a thought occurred to me. "Were you here when that girl was found murdered in that room over there?" I noticed his room also had a view of the room that Richard had rented.

"Yes, I was here."

"Did you see anything?" I asked.

"Not really, no. I saw the police come. The guy who was staying there looked like a bad ass, though."

"So you saw the guy?"

"Yes, I saw him. Big guy, too. I saw him leave the room, then the girl left. Then another girl showed up. Then the guy came back. Then he came running out of the room and the police showed up."

"Both women were in the room at the same time weren't they?" They had to be together at some point for Judy Johnson to kill Amanda Springer.

"Not that I saw, though they could have been, I guess. I remembering thinking how awkward it would be if they ran into each other. This guy must have been a stud to have two good looking women come to his room."

"Well, thanks for your time," I said as I headed to the door. "Would you like a ride to the police station?"

"That would be neighborly of you, thanks," he said as he followed me to the car.

Chapter 22

I tossed and turned all night trying to put the pieces together. I had gone with Billy Banister to the police and they had taken his statement. Barbara Levesque was no longer their main suspect, but that left the question of who murdered Joshua Levesque. But more disturbing than that was Billy's insistence that Judy Johnson and Amanda Springer were not in Richard's room at the same time. If that were true, then it meant that Richard had the opportunity to murder Amanda. I didn't for a minute believe that Richard could be a murderer, but I couldn't think of any logical explanation, hence I spent a restless night.

I gave up trying to sleep and got dressed and made some coffee. I had to go into the office one more time, but I decided to track down Buffy Cunningham. I fumbled around in my wallet and found her business card and punched in her number.

"Hello, Luke," she said. I guess caller ID was working okay.

"Buffy, I've found out something disturbing. Could you meet me for coffee?"

"I have some paperwork to get caught up on, but I can meet you at the coffee shop by the college around eleven this morning,"

"See you there," I said. After she hung up I had the feeling that she was not pleased to hear from me, but maybe I was imagining it.

There was only so much I could do at the office. I had unpacked the boxes that belonged in my office, but I couldn't very well unpack any of the other instructors' materials, but I did have the work-study students deposit the correct packages in the correct offices. Three of the instructors showed up around nine to work on unpacking, and we had an informal department meeting. By the time we finished discussing department business and getting caught up on each other's summer, it was time to head over to the coffee shop.

When I arrived Buffy was pacing outside the shop. She followed me in and we both took our coffee over to a corner table.

"What's up?" she asked. "You sounded upset."

"I talked to one of the residents at the motel. He doesn't like the police, but he told me what he saw."

"Yes, I got a call from the West Hollywood police. Barbara Levesque has been cleared. I thought you believed she was innocent."

"I do, but that's not what is bothering me."

"Then what is it?"

I told her about Billy Banister's observations on the day of Amanda Springer's murder. She paled visibly.

"Did he describe the women?" she asked me.

"No, but we know who the two women are," I said.

"Leave it to me," she replied and seemed to relax. "I'll take care of this,"

"Do you think Richard killed Amanda?" I asked.

"It's beginning to look that way," she answered.

"I don't think he's capable of murder."

"Everyone is capable of murder. You'd be surprised how many murderers seem like sane, well-balanced citizens."

"What would his motive be?" I asked.

"That's a good question. Is he still out there on Cape Cod?"

"Yes," I answered. "You're not going to have him arrested are you?"

"Based on some stoner's testimony? Of course not, but you are not to say anything to him, do you understand?"

"But…"

"If you do I'll have you arrested for interfering with a federal investigation."

"Fine," I said.

"I need to investigate further. I want you to act like nothing has happened. Now I need to go."

We both headed out the door when a thought struck me. How did she know that Billy Bannister was a stoner?

By the time I got off the plane in Boston, I had had enough of flying and the thought of getting on a small plane with propellers wasn't something I wanted to do. I had some credit card points to redeem, so I checked into a nice hotel and used my credits to pay for the room. It was only early afternoon and I thought I'd use the time to do some research at the Boston Historical Society. Any information I could find about early settlements on the outer cape might be helpful. I wasn't prepared for the magnitude of the information in the collection. I knew Richard had been here doing research, and I didn't want to duplicate his efforts, so I decided to give him a call.

"Hey, Luke. What's up?"

"I'm in Boston," I said hoping my voice didn't betray anything. After all I could be talking to a murderer, or at the very least someone who was a suspect and who was unaware that he was. "I'm at the historical society. How far did you get in your search?"

"Just a minute, let me look." I could hear him flipping through his notebook. He told me what sources he had covered.

"Great," I answered. "I'll continue where you left off. Did you find anything of interest?"

"I found a crude map of the village."

"But that's huge!" I said impressed. "That will be the most helpful piece so far. Did it say the name of the village?"

"Tunbridge was the name on the map. I gave the copy to Bert Higgins. He was overjoyed."

"I'm sure he was. So how are you?"

"I'm great. This is a terrific place to be."

"Isn't it," I said. "I'll be there tomorrow." I hung up. Richard sure didn't sound like a killer.

I scanned the digital files and found where Richard left off. There didn't seem to be much order to the files, and I feared looking for information would be like looking for the proverbial needle in a haystack.

Knowing the name of the village didn't help much. I put the name of the town into the search feature of the software, and came up with a ton of hits, but most of the hits seemed to be references to Tunbridge England. It seems that many of the earliest settlers in New England had ties to the English village. While I was reading the files I got a text message from Madison asking me to call her when I got a chance.

It took three hours of research before I found a file folder that looked promising. I pulled out my thumb drive and downloaded the file. I was hopeful that it might contain something useful.

I took my notes and thumb drive and stepped out into the street and called Madison. "What's up?" I asked when I got her on the phone.

"Hi, Luke. I've was cleaning off the blade from the dig when I noticed something as I was examining it under magnification."

"What did you find?" I asked.

"It looks like engraving with the initials JD. It's rusty and worn, but I think that's what it is."

"If it is that could either be the smith who made the blade or it could be the owner. At any rate it's a clue. Good work, Madison."

"Bryan said you'd be coming back tomorrow."

"I'm taking the ferry over. How's Brad, by the way?"

"He's wrapping up his visit to Brookfield and will be here the day after tomorrow."

"Can't wait to see you guys," I said and rang off.

It had been a long day, and I went back to the hotel, ordered room service and went to bed.

I got up early and had breakfast at the hotel bar, hopped on the subway and walked the two blocks to the waterfront. The ferry was a catamaran that was able to leave Boston and arrive in Provincetown in ninety minutes. There was a party atmosphere about the ferry.

Apparently no one was going to Provincetown on business. The passengers were a diverse group, with married day trippers, gays and lesbians on vacation, and the elderly on an outing.

"Whale!" shouted someone out on deck and everyone rushed to the port side of the boat to look. At first there was nothing to see and then suddenly a large whale breached and the air was filled with sounds of wonder."

The morning was clear and our first sight of Provincetown was Pilgrim monument towering over the town. Bryan was at the dock to meet me as the crowd flooded the downtown area. Bryan took my shoulder bag and I dragged my wheeled case up the street to the inn.

"How was California?" he asked.

"Not nearly as nice as here." I gave him the rundown on what was happening at the college.

"So your office is set to go?"

"More or less. I'm sure when I actually go to work in the office I'll discover all the missing items."

"You don't seem to have good luck with offices," he said. "Your old office was hiding a body in the wall, and your new office was almost blown up and set on fire."

Buffy warned me not to tell anyone about Richard's possible guilt in the murder case of Amanda Springer, but I trusted Bryan more than I trusted Buffy Cunningham.

"I did learn something disturbing," I said as we approached the inn.

"What is it?"

"Let me drop off these bags and let's take a walk."

"Sounds serious."

"It is," I said.

"Well, look what got dragged in," said Norma Jean as we walked into the lobby, "Poor Bryan's been pining away without you."

"I doubt that," I said. "I'm sure Bryan has had more than his share of male attention."

"I had to beat them off," he replied.

"What?"

"With a stick," he said and laughed.

"Well," said Norma Jean with a tone that I had come to recognize as a warning. "I got me a supplier. They got good grass up here."

"I don't think," said Bryan, "that anyone has used the term grass since 1970."

"That was a good year," she replied. "Lots of men and lots of dope."

"Lots of men who were dopes, more likely," said Bryan.

"Back then," she reminisced, "a guy knew how to make a girl groan with pleasure."

"No details," I said. "Now if you'll excuse me I need to go unpack."

Chapter 23

Bryan looked at me as we walked along the breakwater, "You don't believe that Richard killed that girl do you?"

"I don't know what to believe anymore," I said. I was being careful not to step on seagull poop as we walked along. "On one hand the eye witness is a known marijuana smoker and he didn't come forward until now. On the other hand he was right about Barbara Levesque not leaving the motel when her husband was murdered."

"It's possible that he didn't see Barbara on that day at all. He could be wrong about that as well as wrong about Richard."

"I hadn't thought about that."

"That's because you always take everyone at face value. I, on the other hand, am a cynical bastard."

"You are many things, but not cynical," I responded. "So what do we do now?"

"First off we can't let Richard know that we suspect him. But in order to clear him, we have to find out who really killed Amanda Springer."

"And Joshua Levesque."

"That too," he agreed. "Though they might or might not be connected."

"They both were members of the Followers."

"As was Richard," Bryan reminded me.

"But he was undercover."

"But still a member as far as the organization is concerned. And he wouldn't be the first undercover agent to sympathize with the group they were investigating.

Making friends and seeing people in their daily life makes it hard to see them as the opposition, so to speak."

We walked to the end of the breakwater and sat down to watch the sun set over the beach. The brilliant red sky signaled another hot and hazy day on the cape.

"Dustin will be devastated if Richard is guilty," I finally said.

"Yes, I believe he will, but let's not jump to conclusions. There is every reason to believe that Richard is innocent. So we are going to do nothing and say nothing."

"Okay," I agreed.

"Wait, you agreed too easily. I know you and you are not going to let this go are you?"

"I'm an anthropologist, I study humanity in all its complexity, and to answer your question, no I am not going to let it go."

It was evening and Provincetown was coming alive. Revelers were taking over the town. The benches outside of the town hall, known as the meat rack, were filling up with those looking for connections. The more sexually adventurous were heading over to the dick dock, whose name is self-explanatory. I was heading to one of the few quiet bars to meet with the Provincetown poets. James Cameron, Buford Chase, and Laurence Stafford were already gathered at a corner table.

"Luke, over here," James waved to me as I entered the bar. I pulled up a chair and sat down. "We were just discussing our writing progress.

"I'm afraid I have been too busy to write this summer."

"But," said James, "just think of all the material you'll have to write about."

"I hadn't thought of it that way."

"If your investigation of the centuries old mysterious death pans out, you could use that for one of your books," added Buford.

"How is the dig going?" asked Laurence.

"So far cellar holes, shell heaps, and broken pottery," I replied. "And of course a few bones."

"Sounds like enough to base a book on," said Buford.

"And then there are the murder cases back in West Hollywood," James reminded everyone.

"There must be a book there," added Buford.

"Enough about me," I said to change the subject. "What are you guys working on?"

"James just published another poem in *Poetry America*," Buford informed the group. Everyone congratulated him. "And now you have material for a book based on a centuries old murder."

"Only if I can make sense of all the pieces," I responded. "What about you?" I said to Laurence.

"I'm almost finished with my next book. I'm way ahead of schedule."

"Your book agent must be happy."

"No book agent for me. I self-publish. There's more money in it."

"Is there?" I asked.

"Do the research," Laurence answered.

"What can I get you, sir?" asked the young waiter who sashayed up to our table.

"A nice cold IPA. And another round for my friends here."

Our literary talk continued until midnight when I excused myself. Before I left I asked James if he would mind sitting down with me later this week. I needed an FBI view of the West Hollywood situation, even if it was from an ex FBI agent.

Heading back to the inn I passed by the meat rack and saw Bryan sitting there on a bench.

"What are you doing out here?"

"Waiting for a hunky looking professor slash model. I think you'll do."

"I'll do most anything for good looking cop types."

"That's what it says on the men's room wall back at the college."

"Then I think you ought to sample the menu when we get back to the inn."

"I think you're right," he answered as we headed back.

Norma Jean and Jenks were already up and having coffee in the lobby when Bryan and I came down for breakfast.

"You boys having a good time?" asked Jenks as we filled our plates up at the buffet.

"You bet," said Bryan.

"It's good to be back," I chimed in.

"How was West Hollywood?" asked Norma Jean as she refilled her coffee cup.

"Hot, dry, and brown. The drought is doing a number on California."

"That's what I like about here," responded Jenks. "Everything is green and lush."

"Winter is another matter," I said. "Cold, dark, and wet."

"It looks so pretty," Norma Jean had never been in snow.

"It looks nice in picture books, but they don't show you what it looks like after a few days. You don't see the slush, the dirt, and the dried salt on your car and on your boots, and you can't feel the bitter, killing cold."

"He doesn't like winter," she said to Jenks unnecessarily.

"Well, my babe here," Jenks pointed to Norma Jean, "wants to go back home, so tomorrow we're heading back."

"Then tonight," Bryan said, "we'll have a little farewell dinner."

"Make it early," replied Norma Jean. "I need my beauty sleep."

"You're going to have to sleep a long time," came Dustin's voice as he entered the dining area followed by Richard.

"Asshole," muttered Norma Jean.

Richard held up a notebook, "Luke, I thought we could compare notes and start looking at the historical aspect of the dig."

"Let's go over there this morning and see if there is anything new that the crew has uncovered, then we can look at our notes. Where's Madison?"

"She's right here," said Madison entering the room. "I overslept."

"You and Brad weren't exactly sleeping last night," said Dustin. "The walls are thin."

"You should talk," she responded.

"Let's meet on the front porch and get over to the dig," I said as I finished my eggs and bacon.

"Anyone want a hit before you go?" Norma Jean held up a freshly rolled joint.

"Put that away," I said.

"Buzz kill," she replied.

Richard and Madison got into the car as I slipped behind the wheel and drove off to the dig site. Richard was riding shotgun and Madison was in the back seat.

"Why do you keep looking at me that way?" asked Richard.

"What way?" I guess I was looking at him trying to picture him as a murderer. While I didn't believe he could be a killer there was that nagging doubt in my head. After all what did I really know about the man? That he was a good student? That he was a former military man? Or that he was Dustin's boyfriend? None of those facts ruled out murder.

"Maybe it's my imagination."

"I'm sure it is," I responded. I guess I'd have to watch myself closely. We drove into the site and headed for the tent. Bert Higgins came over to see us.

"We have some more pottery for you to look at," he said and pointed to a corner of the tent where a table had been set up for the newest finds. "Richard's map has been a great help. We've located the graveyard and as we feared it's lying under the neighbors' cottages.

"It figures," I said. "Didn't they notice any bones when they were digging?"

"The cottages are on pilings, so there wasn't much digging. Plus the water table is higher over there and there wouldn't have been much bone left after three hundred years. We were lucky that the sandy soil over here was dry enough to retard bone decomposition for your mystery man."

"True enough," I agreed. "Let's have a look at the artifacts."

We spent the morning identifying the various artifacts and classifying them. Several items clearly belonged to the later period of the late eighteen hundreds, but the majority of them were consistent with the early colonial period. Among the findings were pieces of earthenware and stoneware, several rusted iron tools, and some hand-forged nails. Nails are rare because much of colonial cabinet making and building were joined by wooden pegs.

"Madison, show me the blade where you think there are initials."

"Over here," she opened the box and unwrapped the blade. "If you take the lighted magnifier and hold the blade at an angle you can see what looks like initials."

I held the blade and moved it under the magnifier and sure enough, I could just make out what appeared to be a J and a D.

"Richard, come take a look at this," I said and gave him the blade.

"I concur," he said as he examined it. "It's hard to make out with the rust and corrosion, but it's definitely a J and D."

I looked at my watch. "I'm meeting a friend for lunch. Carry on. Richard when I get back we will go over our research findings. I think we can begin to work on the narrative soon."

James Cameron was waiting for me when I entered the Mayflower Café. He must have read my mind because he had a notebook and a pen ready for our meeting.

"Good to see you James. Thanks for meeting me."

"You sounded like it was business, so I came prepared," he pointed to his notebook as he spoke.

"How did you know?"

"Years in the FBI helped me to hone my people reading skills. So why don't you tell me what's going on."

"Let's order lunch first," I said. "I'm starving." The truth was I needed a little time to gather my thoughts.

We both ordered a draft and a cheeseburger. The waitress brought our beer and I began to talk. "Here's the thing that's bothering me. There have been two murders of the members of the Followers, a religious cult that wants to create a religious state. So far they are responsible for a demonstration at Cranmore College and then setting up an explosion in the administration building, at least according to a letter that is now missing.

"So which is bothering you? The explosion or the murders?"

"Both really, but one of my graduate students is involved in at least one of the murders."

"The one who was working undercover?"

"Yes, he's one of the best graduate students I have worked with."

"But he was cleared by the FBI wasn't he?"

"Yes, but then as I was looking into the murder of Joshua Levesque I came across an eye witness that was able to support the wife's alibi. I didn't believe she killed her husband. I was there at the motel when he was killed and I knew she was there, but I couldn't swear to it. I was relieved when I uncovered a witness."

"Why didn't he come forward before?"

"He doesn't like the police and he didn't want to become involved." Our burgers arrived and we took the first few bites in silence.

"So you should be pleased that you were able to clear the wife."

"Yes, of course, but then I asked him if he was there when a young member of the Followers was killed. Richard was helping a young woman get away from the cult, but she was a plant because they must have been suspicious of him. The woman disappeared and when he went out to get some food, he came back and there was a different girl in his room and she was dead. And then as he headed out for help he was hit by a car in a hit-and-run situation."

Between bites James had been scribbling in his notebook. "Okay, this is getting complicated."

"According to agent Cunningham, Richard was set up by the Followers."

"That makes sense."

"But we all thought that the first woman, Judy Johnson, brought in the second woman, Amanda Springer, and killed her while Richard was out."

"I see. And you have doubts?"

"According to the eyewitness, Judy Johnson left before Amanda Springer arrived. And Judy Johnson is missing."

"Interesting," he said and sat back and looked at me. "So you think Richard killed the girl?"

"I don't believe it, but the evidence looks like it. The problem is the eye witness has a liking for smoking pot."

"Ah, so his credibility is in question. I think I understand your situation now."

"So what should I do?"

"Finish your lunch and let me think for a few minutes."

We finished our lunch and James closed his notebook.

"It seems," he said, "that there are too many loose ends in this case. You could just leave it all up to agent Cunningham."

I shook my head.

"I didn't think so. In that case here is what you need to check on. First you need to take a look at Amanda Springer. Something seems a little off about her murder. Second take a closer look at the Followers. All you have is a missing letter that links them to the Cranmore explosion."

"I get that," I said.

"And take a look at Levesque. He was murdered for a reason. What seems to be lacking is a strong motive."

"Motive for what?"

"A motive for everything: the explosion, the two murders; how do they tie in?"

"That has been bothering me. Thanks for your help."

"Any time, Luke."

Chapter 24

We were a large group that was gathered for Norma Jean and Jenks's last dinner in Provincetown. It was the height of the summer season, and we had reservations at the Lobster Pot. Several tables had been fitted together to give us room.

"Drinks are on me," said Dustin. I knew of all of us he would miss Norma Jean the most. Their constant sniping at each other was just the way they showed affection.

"A toast," I offered when our drinks arrived. "To friends and to summer." The sentiment was echoed around the table to the sound of clinking glasses."

"I just want to thank everyone," said Jenks holding his glass. "You've taken me in and treated me like one of your family."

"Anyone who can put up with that crazy old lady is okay with us," replied Dustin.

"Asshole," sputtered Norma Jean.

"Hag," said Dustin.

"Children, behave," I warned, "or you get no dessert."

"Buzz kill," she said to me.

"Blake, how are your photos coming along?" I asked to change the subject.

"I've got some great shots of the town and the dunes, but I need some people shots. Would you consider posing for some?"

"Why not?" I said not really sure if I wanted to or not.

"And I still want to do the photo spread of the dig. Do you think you've got enough interesting things for me to photograph?"

"I expect by the end of the week that we'll be finishing up the research and putting together the narrative of Tunbridge Village.

"Tunbridge?"

"Yes, the research that Richard did when he was in Boston indicated that there was a fishing village called Tunbridge sometime in the 1690s."

"What about the murder?" asked Blake.

"I love a good murder," piped up Norma Jean.

"I guess we'll have to call it a centuries old mystery." I couldn't foresee any way to solve it.

"Well, it will still make good reading," said Blake.

"Anyone want another drink?" asked the waiter as he passed out the menus. We all raised our glasses.

It was three o'clock in the morning. Bryan sat up in bed and turned on the light. "What's the matter?" he asked. I had been tossing and turning all night as sleep eluded me.

"I keep going over the murders. It bothers me that Richard might be involved."

"It really isn't up to you to solve any murders. You need to relax and let the police or the FBI or whoever solve the case. It has nothing to do with you."

"But…"

"No buts. Go back to sleep and forget about it."

"I need to talk to Billy Banister again. I'll give him a call." I started to get out of bed.

"It's midnight in California. You'll have to wait until tomorrow afternoon. And does the stoner even have a phone?"

"There are phones in the motel rooms."

"Fine, but it's too early to call and you need some sleep. So do I for that matter."

"Don't you think we should tell Richard that he might be a suspect?"

"In spite of what Buffy Cunningham says, yes I think we should. But not yet."

Richard and I spent the morning comparing notes from our research of Tunbridge Village. Slowly we were able to piece together details of life in 1690s Cape Cod. I had to admire the determination of the early settlers as they faced what seems insurmountable problems. I doubted that any of us would have the fortitude to face what these settlers had to face.

"We've pretty much hit a wall here," said Richard. "Where do we go from here?"

"We still need to check out the historical societies on the outer cape. They may have some documents that might help shed light on Tunbridge. They may be unaware of the value of what they have.

"Where should we look?"

"I think Truro to Eastham is a good place to start. Most of the local historical societies are run by volunteers. I found in the past that they can be very helpful."

"So they are a good source of documentation?"

"Very much so." I looked at my watch. "I have to go make a phone call. Why don't you file these notes, and then we'll break for lunch."

I placed a call to the Sky View Motel. Barbara Levesque answered.

"Luke, how can I thank you," she said over the phone. "You got Billy to support my alibi. I can't thank you enough."

"It was a lucky break. Could you put me through to Billy's room?"

"Sure thing," she said. "Hang on." After a brief pause the phone began to ring and Billy picked up.

"Billy," I said before he could speak. "It's Luke Littlefield."

"Hey man, how you doing?"

"I just wanted to ask you about the two women you saw on the day of the murder. Are you sure that the two women weren't in the hotel room at the same time?"

"I sure am. I thought the guy would get caught if the two women were to meet up. Lucky guy to have a blonde and a redhead on the same day. I hoped his girlfriend wouldn't find out. Must be quite the stud."

"You mean there were three women?

"Yes, I think so, though I didn't see her at first.

"So the blonde left and the redhead went to the room?

"No, it was the other way around. The redhead left and the blonde went into the room."

"And they were never in the room together?"

"Not that I saw, no."

"And what about the third woman?"

"Not sure. Only saw her go in and I didn't see her come out."

"I see. Thanks Billy," I said. "You take care now."

I hung up. Three women? Something was terribly, terribly wrong.

Bryan and Dustin had driven Jenks and Norma Jean to the airport in Boston while Madison, Richard and I were at the dig. I would miss Norma Jean. She always added color and comic relief to the day. Brad had left to return to work in California and our group was getting smaller. Blake would be leaving at the end of the week as soon as he finished the photo shoot at the dig. In the meantime he and Buford had been seeing each other. I've never been a fan of vacation romances because it's hard to say goodbye.

I was sitting in a rocker on the front porch of the inn thinking all these thoughts when Blake Carter came up to me with his camera slung around his neck.

"How about posing for me, Luke."

"Where?"

"Right where you are. There's great light out here and the background of the inn is perfect."

"Is this a photo for the story on the dig?"

"No, why?"

"I'll need to dress up in my professor clothing if it is."

"I don't understand why you think you have to look like a geek to be a professor. I would think a hot looking professor would set you apart."

"The academic world values substance rather than appearance."

"Not in my experience. Conformity maybe."

"Maybe you're right," I admitted.

Blake aimed his camera at me and the flash went off. He showed me the photo on the small screen of his camera. I have to say it was a good picture.

"The camera loves you," he said as he continued to take shots.

"I never understood that. Look at Bryan for example. The man looks like a Greek god yet he never has a good picture taken of him."

"Bryan is one of those people who have three dimensional looks. You see him in 3D, yet the camera only sees him as a flat image and so the photo loses something."

"I think I understand," I said.

"Anyway, I thought I'd start taking more photos at the dig tomorrow, if that's okay."

"I'll let Bert Higgins know, and I'll have my crew stage some of the artifacts. We haven't gotten very far on the history part. I can send you the write-ups later if that works with your deadline."

"I've got until the first of September to turn in the article."

"That's more than enough time," I said. "We'll all be back in school by then."

"There you are," said Bryan as he stepped out onto the porch.

"How was your nap?" I asked

"Refreshing, thank you."

"Did you get Norma Jean and her boyfriend off to the airport?" asked Blake.

"Just in time. The Boston traffic is terrible."

"So unlike greater LA," I said with more than a touch of irony.

"LA traffic you expect. I thought New England would be different."

"There is no such thing in New England as a straight road. Most of the streets are old cow paths." I don't think I ever saw a grid system of streets in Maine when I was growing up.

"I've noticed that, too," added Blake.

"Is it dinner time?" asked Bryan.

"I believe it is. Where shall we go?" I asked.

"Let's just walk around and see what looks good," suggested Blake.

"Dustin and Richard have plans," said Bryan.

"Let's get Madison to go with us. I'm sure she's missing Brad," I said.

"Who wouldn't?" added Bryan with a wink.

Chapter 25

Madison was trying her best to crack open a lobster claw. "This is a lot of work for a little meat."

"Wait until you taste it," I said as I broke off a lobster claw from the bright red crustacean. Madison had never had fresh North Atlantic lobster before.

"If I can ever get the meat out," she sighed.

"Just follow my lead," I said as I took up the nut cracker and cracked the claw, fished out the claw meat with a pick and dipped the morsel in melted butter.

"Don't worry," added Bryan. "It took me a while to get the hang of it, too."

Madison cracked open her claw, fished out the meat, speared it with a fork, and dipped it in butter. She put the meat in her mouth and closed her eyes. "Oh, my God! This is delicious."

"Told you," I said.

"These claws look different," she added as she picked up the second claw.

"That one is the crusher claw, used to crack open shells, the first one was the pincher claw, used to tear the meat of the prey," I replied.

"I'm surprised Brad hasn't initiated you into the joys of seafood," said Bryan.

"He's not a fish eater," she replied. "But that's going to change!"

"He's coming back here tomorrow?" I asked.

"Yes, he should be here by noon. When are you two going back to West Hollywood?"

"Bryan has to go back to work on Monday. I'm going to fly back with him and get the department ready for the fall semester."

"I can't wait to teach and be a part of the department."

"I'm looking forward to having you and Richard in the department, but I really want to wrap up the work here first."

"How much longer do you think the dig will go on?"

"I think they've done as much as they could. We'll catalogue the last few artifacts as they come in, and then begin writing up the narrative for the historical society."

"How's the research going?" asked Bryan.

"I've got a few more documents to read through and some visits to the local historical societies." I twisted off the tail of my lobster and opened the thorax and scooped out the green liver.

"What is that?" asked Madison with a look of distaste.

"It's tomalley, mostly the liver."

"It looks gross."

"Lots of people refuse to eat it, but it's their loss. Try it," I encouraged.

She took a spoon, scooped out the tomalley, gave it a dubious look and took a taste. "It's actually good."

"Of course," I replied. "Now let's move on to the tail meat. And there's strawberry shortcake as the featured dessert."

Saturday afternoon Bryan and I were busy packing up to go back to California. Bryan had to go back to work, and I would be flying back here after a few days to finish up the project. I knew I would miss Bryan, but it would be only for two weeks or so before I returned to California for good.

Richard Hall's guilt or innocence was weighing on my mind, so I knew I needed to talk to Billy Banister one more time. I picked up my phone and dialed the Sky View Motel.

Barbara Levesque answered the phone. "Hi, Barbara. It's Luke Littlefield. I'd like to talk to Billy."

"Oh, Luke. Something dreadful has happened. Billy's dead!"

"Dead?"

"Yes, we found him in his room. He overdosed."

"What do you mean he overdosed?"

"They found a syringe filled with heroine in his room."

"Billy smoked weed," I said confused. "But he was dead set against hard drugs."

"That's what we all thought. But the police found drugs hidden in his room."

"I'm coming to West Hollywood tomorrow. I'll be stopping by sometime this week."

"I'll look forward to thanking you in person," she said.

I hung up the phone. Something was terribly wrong.

The flight to Los Angeles was uneventful and we were back in West Hollywood by the end of the day. The first thing Bryan did was go to the shop and check in with Brenda Johnson, the clerk he had hired to cover for Norma

Jean. Brenda was a graduate student who was taking a semester off and was grateful for the opportunity for work.

"Dr. Littlefield, is that you?" she asked when I entered the shop with Bryan. I hadn't bothered to dress up in professor drag.

"Of course it is," I snapped. Realizing I had been sharp and was probably suffering from jet lag I smiled.

"You look different without the glasses. And your hair is different."

"Yes, I know."

"You're the guy on the poster!" She was pointing to the full length posters that Norma Jean had made up as "vintage" images.

"It's just a coincidence," I said but I was sure she didn't believe me. Bryan came to my rescue.

"Has Norma Jean been in?" he asked.

"She came in this morning and worked on the books. We've had a lot of sales. Also she left you some memos about estate sales that you might like to attend."

"I guess it wouldn't hurt to increase inventory. How have sales been?" asked Bryan.

"We've been busy. And that Victorian wardrobe sold for full price." Brenda was looking at me as she was talking and looking at the poster too.

"Any gossip," I said to Brenda, "linking me to that poster would have unfortunate consequences, if you get my meaning."

"Of course," she answered to my veiled threat. I didn't explain that the consequences would be mine.

"Well, look what the east wind blew in," Norma Jean said as she entered the shop. "Tweedle Dee and Tweedle

Dum." She was dressed in a bright red jogging suit with rhinestones that spelled out "Hot Mama" on the front.

"Nice suit," I said.

"Yes, it is," she answered missing the irony in my voice. "I bedazzled it myself."

"It shows."

"Where's Jenks?" asked Bryan.

"I tired him out and he's run out of blue pills. Insurance only pays for four of those a month. What the hell are they thinking? A young chick like me needs action."

"Too much information," I said through gritted teeth.

"Agent Cunningham was in yesterday," she said thankfully changing the subject. "She wanted to know if you guys were still in Provincetown."

"What did you tell her?" asked Bryan.

"I didn't tell her anything. I don't like her. She's a…" and here Norma Jean used a crude word that was so highly inappropriate that I won't repeat it.

"I don't think anyone likes the woman. But she has a job to do," responded Bryan. "Not that I don't agree with you. Now if everything is okay here, Luke and I should get over to the campus."

The next day I made my way over to the Sky View Motel. Barbara Levesque was at the front desk and on the phone when I entered the office. She gave me a wave and a smile while she finished with what I gathered was a phone reservation.

"Dr. Littlefield, I can't thank you enough," she came out from behind the counter and gave me a hug. "If it wasn't for you convincing Billy to come forward, I'd still be in jail."

"You're welcome," I said. "Would you mind giving me some information?"

"Anything for you," she said and I had the feeling she wasn't limiting herself to just information.

"Tell me about the Followers." I watched her face go from determination to resignation.

"Yes, I suppose you will want to know everything."

"We've had two murders and I'm not so sure that Billy's overdose was accidental."

"You think his death is connected?"

"If nothing else his death is convenient. He's the only witness to your innocence and he was present the day Amanda Springer was killed."

"Why do you care about any of this?"

"Because I have a friend who may be involved and I need answers."

"Very well. But I think we need to go somewhere else and talk. It's a long story. I'll get my sister to watch the office."

Chapter 26

It was a warm day but there was a breeze and as I looked around at the motel I saw several inhabitants had chosen to forego air conditioning and had opened their windows to the clear air. I followed Barbara across the courtyard of the motel to a small outside pool area set up with umbrella shaded tables and chairs. There was no one else at the pool. We took a seat at one of the shaded tables and Barbara began her tale.

"We had a group of the Followers stay here for several days last year. Two of the members struck up a friendship with Joshua and before I knew it he was telling me all about this group who wanted to establish a new world order."

"Didn't that sound a little crazy?" I asked.

"It did at first, but listening to them after a while they began to make sense. Mostly they talked about crime and how crime could be wiped out with God's help. We began to go to their meetings and pretty soon Joshua joined the inner circle, and then he took a leadership role in the local group. I went along with it and pretended to care, but I knew it was a sham."

"But you did become a leader?"

"I attended the meetings with my husband, and I pretended to be a leader to keep an eye on my husband. He had a roving eye, but The Followers were a little too out there for me."

"Did you know about the bombing at Cranmore?"

"I can tell you that the Followers had nothing to do with that. For all their craziness they are a peaceful group."

"But the group claimed responsibility for the bombing," I said.

"Someone sent a letter claiming the Followers did it, but they didn't send the letter. The group was set up. As you know we all have alibis. We were at a meeting."

"What about the protest at the college?"

"We received an email telling us that there would be a peaceful demonstration at the college. We were going to have a pray-in and hand out some literature. Some young men appeared and pretended to be members from the Los Angeles group and instigated the unrest. Someone began to throw rocks. It just got out of hand."

"You think the group has been set up?"

"Yes, I think another group is trying to discredit the Followers."

"Are you still a member?" I asked.

"God, no. They may be peaceful, but they are still crazy."

"So tell me about Billy," I said to change the subject.

"One of our housekeeping workers went in to clean the room and found Billy dead."

"Could I see the room?"

"I don't see why not. The police have already been through it."

Barbara gave me the pass key to Billy's room. I unlocked the door and ducked under the yellow police tape that was still strung across the door. The room looked much as I'd seen it when I first talked to Billy. There were 1970s posters around the room as well as antidrug signs and antidrug pamphlets. There were also lots of materials on legalizing pot. Billy, I concluded, didn't see pot as a gateway drug. I found no computer or cell phone, so I thought Billy was likely to keep a notebook somewhere, but I was sure the police would have found it if that were true.

I tried to think of any place that the police might have failed to check. Ceiling tiles and toilet tank would be the obvious places to look, as were chair cushions and mattresses. I took a seat and looked about the room trying hard to think of a hiding place. I looked around the room and saw my reflection in the Television screen. I didn't think Billy was the TV type. That gave me an idea. I got up and walked over to the TV set and checked the back. Several of the screws were missing and the remaining ones were loose. I took out my pocket knife and carefully removed the remaining screws. Bingo! There was a small notebook taped to the inside back cover. I took the notebook and slipped it into my pocket, exited the room and closed the door.

I was about to get into my car when a tall man stepped out of the shadows and flashed a badge at me.

"Dr. Littlefield, we need to talk."

"What's this about and who are you?"

"I'm Special Agent Connelly, FBI. We need you to stand down."

"Stand down? I don't understand."

"You're looking into the Followers' murders. We need you to stop."

"Why?"

"Let's just say it's in your best interest."

"You guys should have thought of that before Agent Cunningham got me involved. One of my friends may be involved, and I'm not going to just sit back."

"Agent Cunningham shouldn't have gotten you involved. I know she can be a bit headstrong, but you could be in danger if you don't back off."

"Not going to happen," I said and began to walk away.

"I was afraid you were going to say that. Very well there are a few things I need to tell you." And what I heard next sent chills down my spine. "So if you are still stubborn then I've got a job for you to do."

"If it will clear Richard, then count me in."

Bryan stopped in at my office as he was making the rounds of the campus. I had just about unpacked my last box and was setting up my computer.

"Glad to be back?" he asked as he practically threw himself down on one of my chairs.

"I'd rather be back in Provincetown to tell the truth."

"Me, too. But at least you get to go back."

"Yes, but without you it's going to be all work."

"Well, you can have those great conversations with the Provincetown poets. And Dustin and Richard will be there."

"And Madison and hunky Brad Tanner who'll be flying in again.," I added.

"So how did your visit to the motel go?"

"I found this," I said as I handed him the notebook.

"What's this?"

"It looks like a journal that Billy kept."

"Anything interesting?"

"Not really. His handwriting is almost illegible. It's taking me a while to read through it."

"Don't you think you should turn it over to the police?"

"I met with an FBI agent when I was over there. He rattled me so much that I forgot I had it."

"FBI? Why did you meet with him?"

"It wasn't my idea." Then I told Bryan what the FBI told me.

He gave out a long whistle when I finished with my tale. "You be careful."

"Count on it," I said.

Agent Connelly met me at the coffee shop around the corner. We took our coffees off to a table away from everyone. I passed him the notebook.

"I found it in the back of the TV. Apparently the police didn't look there."

"They were more interested in looking around for drugs than cleaning up the room of a dead drug user."

"I've marked the more interesting pages. Billy seems to have written down details each day. Most of the stuff is crushingly boring, until you get to page twenty-nine."

"This is difficult to read," Connelly said as he squinted at the pages.

"It takes a few minutes to get used to his penmanship and abbreviations. But then it gets easier."

"Does this say what I think it says?" he asked after reading page twenty-nine.

"Yes, it does."

"Hot damn! Okay we're doing a new plan. Are you up for it?"

"I'm ready," I said, though I wasn't quite as sure as my spoken words.

Norma Jean had spiked her fake blonde hair with streaks of pink, probably to match her pink tank top and short shorts. She and I were sitting in the Coffee Break Café. We were getting all types of odd looks. "I think I need to break up with Jenks."

"Why?" I asked. "I thought he was the one."

"He's married."

"He was married last week, too."

"Yes, but he told me his wife was gaga." She made a twirling motion at her head with her finger."

"And?"

"And, he might have exaggerated. I don't think she's as gaga as he said."

"I see. And what makes you think that?"

"We ran into one of Jenks's friends and he acted strange when I was introduced."

"That could be for any number of reasons, not the least of which is your hair," I said pointing to the offending pink streaks.

"I'm totally rocking this hair. I need you to do something for me."

"I'm afraid to ask."

"I need you to go to the nursing home and check out this woman."

"I don't think so."

"But I need to know," she said as her eyes filled with tears.

"Fine," I relented. "Where is she?"

"Sunny Isles Retirement Home over in the canyon."

"I've been looking for you," said a voice. I looked up to see Buffy Cunningham standing behind me."

"Well," said Norma Jean, "I should go." She looked at Buffy as she got up to leave. "See you next Tuesday, bitch."

"Next Tuesday?" asked Buffy looking confused. "What's next Tuesday?"

"Never mind," I said. "What can I do for you?"

"I thought I'd just check in with you because I've have reached a wall in my investigation. I was wondering if you'd had any new insights."

"Me? What have I to do with anything?" Buffy was clearly interested in finding out if I knew anything. I wasn't sure what to tell her at this point since I had no proof. I decided to gather more information before talking to her.

"Your friend Richard is a person of interest. I thought maybe you had some thoughts? It looks like the evidence points to him. Do you think he could be guilty?"

"I don't believe he did it, but I've been too busy with the dig and getting ready for the fall term to do any type of digging. I'm not sure why I'm involved in any of this and I'd like to stay out of it if possible."

"Good," she said and seemed to relax. "Leave it up to the FBI."

I wanted to tell her that I was sick of the FBI, but I held my tongue.

Chapter 27

The Sunny Isles Retirement Home was one of those institutional complexes that try to hide their real purpose behind a façade of landscaping and innovative architecture. But once you walk inside the hospital smell and the wide corridors tell its real purpose. I walked up to the reception desk.

"I'm here to see Mildred Carter." I knew if I asked about a patient they wouldn't give me any information because of patient confidentiality. However, if I came for a visit I would be shown in and then I could make an assessment for myself.

"Carter? Let me see," the receptionist hit some keys on her computer. "Sorry, I don't have a   Mildred Carter here."

"I was sure my aunt was here," lying was becoming easier and not something I'm proud of either.

She hit some more keys to do a global search. "I'm sorry to tell you, but Mildred passed away over a year ago."

"I see," I said. "Thank you." Jenks had some explaining to do.

When I arrived home I saw Norma Jean's red mustang parked outside. Entering the house I heard voices coming out of the kitchen. I forgot that this was veggie delight night when Norma Jean and Dustin invaded my kitchen, but I knew Dustin was still out on the cape. I recognized the voice to be that of Jenks.

"What's going on?" I asked.

"I'm making black bean burgers and I asked Jenks to help me since Dustin isn't here."

"Well, I've had a long day and could use a beer. Why don't you join me out on the porch, Jenks. Norma Jean is capable of making dinner by herself."

"Sounds good," he said. "I'm really not much help."

"He really isn't," piped up Norma Jean.

I grabbed two beers out of the refrigerator and we headed out to the porch.

"What's new?" asked Jenks once we were seated.

"I was just out to Sunny Isles to pay my respects to your wife. Imagine my surprise when I found out she had been dead for over a year."

"I can explain," he said turning very pale.

"I doubt it," I said. "But give it a shot."

"A widower with some money is a target for every widow over sixty. I always say my wife is alive just to be clear that marriage is out of the question. When I met Norma Jean I wasn't sure where the relationship was going. After a few weeks it was too late to tell the truth. I'd been lying too long. You have to know that I really like her."

"And you have to know that she's planning to break up with you because she thinks your wife is still alive. So here's your choice. You can tell her, or I can tell her. But if I tell her I can guarantee that it wouldn't end well for you."

"I understand."

"So I suggest you go in there and tell her that I send my regrets, but that I've been called away and that you have something important to discuss with her." I called Bryan and told him we wouldn't be dining at home.

The end was in sight. I took a deep breath and called Special Agent Connelly and then Agent Cunningham. It was time to work with the FBI if I wanted to clear Richard. I agreed to meet Buffy Cunningham for drinks at one of the large chain restaurants near the mall. Buffy was already seated and halfway through her martini when I arrived and was led over to her table.

"Good to see you, Luke," she said but I could tell she just as soon spit at me.

"And you also." I was getting this lying thing down pretty well. A waiter appeared and placed a martini in front of me. I looked up at the waiter with a shock of recognition. He nodded to me and moved away.

"You said you might have some information about the murders that might help solve the case."

"Maybe, but it's just a theory, but when an anthropologist studies divergent cultures we always look for common denominators."

"Common denominators? What are you talking about?"

"What is the one thing the two murders have in common?"

"No idea. Why don't you tell me?"

"It's you, of course. You're the common denominator."

"Don't be an ass, I'm the fucking FBI."

"It took me awhile to put together the pieces, but when I did all the evidence pointed to you."

"Interesting theory, but what motive would I have?"

"We'll get there," I said. "But first let's take a look at a few things. First of all the Followers are a group of religious whack jobs, but they have no history of violence. Their peaceful demonstration at the college turned ugly because of outside agitators. And the bombing of the college? All that linked them to the bombing was a letter that claimed responsibility, which conveniently disappeared. You did a sloppy job on that one because they all had alibis. Next time you need to do a better job."

"You're crazy."

"Let's take a closer look at Joshua Levesque's murder. You went to meet him that night after you flirted with him shamelessly. You claim he never showed up and then was found dead. The one thing that puzzled me was that his feet were cut up with glass, but there was no glass on the ground anywhere in the park. According to the lab it was car window glass. Very strange until I remembered seeing your car parked on the street by the park."

"My car? What the hell does my car have to do with it?" Buffy signaled the waiter for another drink, which he brought over. The drink was beginning to affect her which made me think she had had a few before she arrived at the restaurant.

"I thought it strange at the time because your windows were down. One does not leave their windows down in that neighborhood, which makes me think that one of the windows was missing, maybe kicked out. Roll down all the windows and no one would guess that there was a missing window."

"I suppose you think I murdered Amanda Springer as well?"

"Actually yes. Here again it was your sloppiness that gave you away. It was you at the motel who killed that girl. And it was you and Judy Johnson who tried to run over Richard, and I'm going to guess that Judy Johnson will turn up dead very soon since she has served her purpose.

But what is really interesting is that you didn't realize that someone saw you go into the motel. He told me about seeing two women go into Richard's motel room. I thought they were Amanda Springer and Judy Johnson. I was worried that it looked like Richard could be the murderer. But on my second interview with Billy he told me about the blonde and the red head. Amanda was a red head, but Judy had dark hair, so there really were three women involved. You're the only blonde in this scenario.

"And then there's Billy. Billy was very antidrug, yet he died of an overdose. I think you killed him because you were afraid he'd say something to give you away. But you were too late."

"And the motive? What possible motive would I have?"

"That's the easiest mystery to solve. You've been on probation with the FBI. If you could break up a terrorist group, like the Followers, you'd redeem yourself. The problem is that they're not terrorists and you're incompetent."

"You think you're very clever, don't you? But I've got a gun pointed at you under the table and we're going for a little ride."

"Well, don't look now, but the waiter standing behind you has a gun pointed at your head."

Special Agent Douglas Connelly was still wearing the waiter uniform when we finished up statements, reports and the tons of paperwork needed to put away Buffy Cunningham. One murder would be enough to put her away for life. Three murders and she didn't have a chance in hell of ever seeing daylight. The FBI frowns upon dirty agents and if I had to guess, I'd say her survival time in prison was likely to be short.

"Luke, how about a drink?" asked Doug Connelly. After the events of the day we were on a first name basis. "There's a great little pub around the corner."

"I could use one," I said. I tried to act cool, but the adrenalin rush I experienced helping bring Cunningham down was beginning to wear thin, and I was feeling a little shaky.

"It goes without saying that you were a great help to us in bringing her down," said Doug as we sat in the pub with mugs of stout in front of us.

"I just happened to be in the right places at the right time. If Agent Max Bailey hadn't shown Bryan and me the probation file on Buffy, I probably wouldn't have been as observant. What I said about common denominators is true. In this case I was the common denominator observing the details of the case."

"Just so you know, we typically don't share our files with civilians, but we had to warn you not to trust her. And we did plenty of background checking on you and Bryan."

"And I appreciate being trusted and I'm proud to help out."

"Well, it worked out for us, too. Have you called Bryan yet?"

"I don't think I want to tell him in a phone call. It would be better in person."

"True, but you might want to give him a heads up before the media gets hold of the story."

"I never thought of that. Can you keep my name out of it? I don't think the college would appreciate my role in all this."

"I think we can do that, yes. So what are your plans now?"

"I'm going to wrap up my work at Cranmore and head out to Cape Cod and finish my report on the life and artifacts of colonial life on the cape."

"I always miss the action," pouted Norma Jean when I told her the story. She and Jenks were with Bryan and me at the Roma having dinner. They were able to work through Jenks's deception, though I didn't know the details.

"So you're going back to the cape tomorrow?" asked Jenks.

"Yes, I want to finish up my part of the dig and then have a few days' off before the fall term starts."

"Are you going, Bryan?" asked Norma Jean.

"Unfortunately I have to stay here and work. I've already used up too many days."

"It won't take me long to finish up, I don't think. Richard and Madison have been tracking down research leads."

"Richard must be relieved that he's clear of any suspicion," observed Norma Jean.

"I talked to him this morning," said Bryan. "He's very grateful and looking forward to the fall term at Cranmore."

"He and Madison working for me in the anthropology department is something I'm looking forward to as well," I added.

"What about that bitch," asked Norma Jean. "I hope she rots in jail."

"From what I understand she's had a complete psychotic break," I answered.

"No surprise there," agreed Bryan.

"So let's have a toast," said Jenks. "Onward and upward!"

"Onward and upward!" we all echoed.

Chapter 28

Dustin and Richard met me at Boston's Logan Airport and needless to say both of them wanted all the details of Buffy Cunningham's arrest. The traffic to Provincetown was heavy, but once we were in Truro the traffic eased up. I always love the last few miles into Provincetown where the road to town narrows between sand dunes that threaten to swallow up the road.

Innkeepers Bruce Wilson and David Preston were there to greet me and had my room ready. They had heard about my adventures with Buffy Cunningham and wanted more details. They bribed me with a bottle of wine, and I gave them an animated account of Buffy's arrest.

Brad and Madison, along with Dustin and Richard, treated me to dinner at the Lobster Pot. We sat near the windows and had a view of the town beach out back of the restaurant. Once we were settled and had drinks in our hand, I was ready for a progress report on the dig.

"Professor Higgins and his crew are wrapping up the dig," Madison informed me.

"They seemed to have done as much as they could. The rest of the site is on private land, but it's unlikely to have more than a few graves on it," added Richard.

"How about historical research?" I asked.

Madison and Richard looked at each other. Richard took up the narrative. "We visited several local historical societies and found very little."

"Until we got to Wellfleet," broke in Madison.

"At the Wellfleet Historical Society we found a diary from 1690 written by one of the residents of Old

Tunbridge," continued Richard. "Madison spent a day digitizing the entries. I think you need to read it yourself."

"It will answer a lot of questions," added Madison.

"I hope so," I said. "I'd like to finish the narrative and relax for a few days before the fall term."

"I can't wait for the fall term," said Madison. "I'm going to be a real anthropologist."

"Me, too," said Richard.

"You two are already anthropologists," I said. "But now you'll have jobs."

"And we can settle down," said Brad taking Madison's hand.

"And now," said Richard putting his arm around Dustin, "we can all settle down."

The waitress appeared with steaming lobster dinners for all. Summer doesn't get much better than that.

Fog had rolled in overnight and there was a chill in the air. Visibility was limited, but there was something mystical about the atmosphere. I had breakfast and a second cup of coffee and decided to take a walk and enjoy the early morning before I hunkered down to research and write.

It was early and hardly anyone was out and about. Commercial Street was deserted and stood in contrast to the activity of midday. There were a few early patrons at the Post Office Cabaret as I walked by and I spotted James Cameron having coffee. He looked out the window and waved me inside.

"Luke, good to see you," he said. "Have a seat. Coffee is on me."

"Thanks, I think I will."

"What are you doing out so early?"

"Just enjoying a walk in the fog and having downtown to myself."

"It is quite a contrast. You should be here in November when all the tourists are gone."

"No thanks. I'm allergic to winter."

"I've heard about your adventures with the FBI. Now tell me you don't have material for a book."

"Yes, I have to admit that it has given me the plot for my next crime novel, though I'm not sure it's believable. Buffy Cunningham was very sloppy about everything."

"Buffy Cunningham is a psychopath. Being clever isn't one of her strengths."

"What I don't understand is why the FBI didn't clue in on her earlier."

"According to my sources," here James winked at me, "they had their suspicions. When she involved you in her plot that was the tip off. She knew that any FBI agent that she involved would add two and two together. She figured an academic like you would be too dense to see through her plot."

"She was wrong," I said. "I'll be finishing up my research here in a few days. I just want to thank you for including me as a member of the Provincetown Poets."

"You are very welcome. Our membership is for life and that means you have to come back here to Provincetown on a regular basis."

"I'm already planning next summer's vacation here. Hopefully I'll have a new book out by then."

"We'll be looking forward to reading it," said James. The town was beginning to get busy and the sun was trying to burn off the fog. I said my goodbyes and headed back to the inn to collect my gear and head out to the dig.

"Good morning," said Madison who was already at work doing a final inventory of the artifacts and organizing them for distribution. Some artifacts would go to Cranmore's collection with the hope of one day establishing a campus museum. Other artifacts would go to the Provincetown Historical Society.

"Good morning," I answered. "Where's Richard?"

"He's out in the field with Professor Higgins. The digital files are on the thumb drive on your work table over there. The team is cleaning up the site and mapping the foundations. Which of these artifacts are going to Cranmore?"

"Anything that is a duplicate will go with us. One of a kind artifacts will go to the historical society."

"That's fair, I guess."

I took out my laptop, fired it up and plugged in the thumb drive. The file was marked as "Charity Brown's Journal. The files consisted of pages scanned from an old book publish in the 1880s as a transcription from a hand-written journal dated 1691. According to Madison the original journal could not be found and this was printed locally for the Wellfleet historical celebration of 1885.

The file was quite large and I hunkered down for a long session. Some of the passages were interesting, discussing meal preparations and visitors to the family, along with descriptions of fishing catches. Local gossip was also interesting, but the real discovery that Richard and Madison had made was in the fact that Charity Brown lived in Tunbridge and moved to Wellfleet after the little fishing village was destroyed by fire.

The editor of the book had written notations along with excerpts of the journal, often filling in details not evident in the original passages. These scholarly notations were footnoted and would be helpful in extended research later. I planned to have Richard, as our new department researcher, make a thorough study.

It was several hours later when I stumbled upon the most significant passage of the journal. It contained an account of the suicide of Tunbridge's clergyman. The notation read as follows:

> *Prior to the destruction of Tunbridge Village, the population, then a collection of twenty-six families, had been dealing with the unexpected death of Reverend Josiah Babbage. Babbage had apparently committed suicide and had left his flock to deal with the aftermath. John Dutton, a leader in the community, had discovered Babbage's body as it lay in the back of the small chapel. Dutton, much to the relief of the villagers, had undertaken the preparation of the body for burial by himself. Babbage could not be buried in consecrated ground, so he was buried outside the village by the crossroads, a traditional burial place for suicides in*

England. Around the time of the burial, a band of marauding Indians from the south attacked the local Indian village and burned the houses of Tunbridge Village. Gathering up what they could, the villagers, under the leadership of John Dutton, settled in Wellfleet.

"Go find Professor Higgins," I said to Madison. "We've solved the mystery."

"Amazing," remarked Bert Higgins as we all packed up the artifacts and records of the dig. "All this was in one obscure book?"

"Yes, it solved three mysteries," I said as I packed up my laptop and the research notes I had worked on. "We know how the village burned down and whose bones we dug up. Reverend Babbage was buried at the crossroads as a suicide. The bones are consistent with a male of that age."

"And we know he wasn't a suicide," said Bert.

"There must have been some type of disagreement," I said speculating on the possible motive for murder. "The blade we found with the initials JD most likely belong to John Dutton. The fact that he undertook the preparation of the body and oversaw the burial is a good way to hide the true cause of death. The villagers were most likely relieved that they didn't have to deal directly with the death. A very clever cover up."

"What are we going to do with the bones?" asked Madison.

"Shouldn't we reinter them?" asked Richard.

"I've already contacted the town authorities," I answered. "Since we have a name and he was an early settler, the town has agreed to bury him in the town graveyard."

"It seems a shame," though," said Bert Higgins, "that John Dutton got away with murder, literally."

"Not for long," I said. "According to the records he died of drowning at sea less than a year later."

"Don't mess with the Universe," said Madison.

"Amen," added Richard.

Epilogue

It was the night before the start of the fall term and I was having a dinner party. Dustin and Norma Jean were in the kitchen preparing a vegetarian feast. Bryan, in defiance, was out in the backyard grilling burgers and ribs with the help of Jenks.

Madison and Brad were setting up a table and chairs in the backyard for dining, and Richard and I were mixing drinks for everyone.

"Looks like a party," said a voice as Special Agent Douglas Connelly stepped into the backyard.

"Doug," I said, "good to see you. Would you like a drink?" He looked at his watch.

"I'm officially off duty, so yes, I would. A nice dry martini if you have it."

"Coming right up," said Richard as he reached for the shaker.

"What brings you around?" asked Bryan leaving the grilling to shake Doug's hand.

"I have some news. Buffy Cunningham finally confessed to all three murders."

"That's great news," said Richard. "She almost landed me in jail permanently."

"That's where she'll be permanently," Doug took the martini from Richard. "So what's the occasion?"

"It's the beginning of the fall term. Richard and Madison are joining the anthropology department and of course Bryan will have his hands full as security chief when the freshmen hit the campus tomorrow."

Bryan gathered up the burgers and ribs and Norma Jean and Dustin brought out lentil loaf and tofu scramble, along with a Greek salad. Bryan fished out baked potatoes wrapped in foil from the hot coals and dinner was ready.

"A toast," I offered. "On to new adventures!"

"On to new adventures!" echoed everyone.

The End

Made in the USA
San Bernardino, CA
09 December 2015